D1025413

JOURNEY TO THE ALAMO

BOOK ONE

JOURNEY TO THE ALAMO

Melodie A. Cuate

Texas Tech University Press

The paper used in this book meets the minimum requirements of
ANSI/NISO Z 39.48-1992 (R1997).

Illustrations by Lindsay Starr

Library of Congress Cataloging-in-Publication Data
Cuate, Melodie A.
Journey to the Alamo / Melodie A. Cuate.
p. cm. — (Mr. Barrington's mysterious trunk ; bk. 1)
Summary: When the new seventh-grade history teacher brings a mysterious trunk
to class, Jackie, Hannah, and her brother Nick find themselves transported to the Alamo,
where they experience the famous siege first-hand.
ISBN-13: 978-0-89672-592-8 (lithocase : alk. paper)
ISBN-10: 0-89672-592-8 (lithocase : alk. paper) 1. Alamo (San Antonio, Tex.)—
Siege, 1836—Juvenile fiction. 2. Texas—History—Revolution, 1835-1836—Juvenile fic-
tion. [1. Alamo (San Antonio, Tex.)—Siege, 1836—Fiction. 2. Texas—History—Revolu-
tion, 1835-1836—Fiction. 3. Time travel—Fiction. 4. Schools—Fiction.] I. Title. II.
Series: Cuate, Melodie A. Mr. Barrington's mysterious trunk ; bk. 1.
PZ7.C8912Jo 2006
[Fic]—dc22   2006011964

Printed in the United States of America
06 07 08 09 10 11 12 13 14 / 9 8 7 6 5 4 3 2 1
TS
Texas Tech University Press
Box 41037
Lubbock, Texas 79409-1037 USA
800.832.4042
ttup@ttu.edu
www.ttup.ttu.edu

To all the brave men
who gave their lives at the Battle of the Alamo,
and to my husband, Tony, and
my daughter, Erica.

᪥

CONTENTS

❧❦

THE HISTORICAL CHARACTERS

~≍≍~

Allen, James (1815–1901): He left the Alamo as a messenger the night before the Battle of the Alamo on March 5, 1836. Later, he served in the military during the Battle of San Jacinto.

Bowie, James (1796–1836): He was a colonel in the Texas volunteer army. He shared command of the Alamo with Travis until he became ill. Bowie died during the Battle of the Alamo.

Crockett, David (1786–1836): Well-known as a frontiersman and U.S. congressman, Crockett came to Texas in 1835. He had dreams of starting a new life in Texas. He died during the Battle of the Alamo.

Dickinson, Susannah (1814–1883): She was married to Almaron Dickinson, an artillery officer in the Texas army. Susannah and her young daughter survived the

Battle of the Alamo. She carried the message of the fall of the Alamo to Sam Houston.

Dickinson, Angelina (1834–1869): She was a small child during the Battle of the Alamo. Travis gave her his cat's-eye ring. Angelina and her mother were released by the Mexican army several days after the battle.

Esparza, Francisco (1833–1887): He was the son of Gregorio Esparza and the younger brother of Enrique Esparza. His Uncle Francisco served in the Mexican army.

Esparza, Enrique (1828–1917): He was the son of Gregorio Esparza, an Alamo defender. He survived the Battle of the Alamo and told about it in his later life.

Fannin, James (1804–1836): He was the commander of the Goliad forces and was unable to go to the aid of the Alamo defenders. Fannin was killed in the Goliad Massacre.

Fuqua, Galba (1819–1836): He rode into the Alamo with the Gonzales Volunteers. Galba was among the youngest of the defenders and died during the Battle of the Alamo.

Gaston, John (1819–1836): He arrived to the Alamo with the Gonzales Volunteers on March 1, 1836. John was among the youngest of the defenders and died during the Battle of the Alamo.

Joe (1813–?): He was Travis's slave. Joe survived the Battle of the Alamo and accompanied Susannah Dickinson on her journey to find Sam Houston.

King, William (1820–1836): He rode into the Alamo with the Gonzales Volunteers. William was the youngest defender to die during the Battle of the Alamo.

Loysoya, Toribio (1808–1836): He was a member of Captain Juan Seguín's company of *Tejanos* at the Alamo. Toribio died during the Battle of the Alamo.

McGregor, John (1808–1836): He was originally from Scotland and served as an artilleryman at the Alamo. During the siege, McGregor played the bagpipes to entertain the men. He died during the Battle of the Alamo.

Santa Anna, Antonio Lopez de (1794–1876): He was the president of Mexico and the commander of the Mexican army during the Texas Revolution.

Seguín, Juan (1806–1890): He organized a company of *Tejanos* to support the Texas Revolution. Seguín left the Alamo as a messenger before the Battle of the Alamo and led his men during the Battle of San Jacinto. He held a burial service for the fallen defenders of the Alamo.

Travis, William Barret (1809–1836): He was the commander of the Alamo defenders and died during the Battle of the Alamo.

Theodore Gentilz, "Fall of The Alamo," oil painting, ca. 1885.
Courtesy of the Daughters of the Republic of Texas Library.

JOURNEY TO THE ALAMO

Shimmering, glittery,
smoke swirls 'round your head.
Time twists backwards
on the wisp of a thread.
With a heart full of courage,
crossed fingers for luck,
hold your breath,
take a journey,
lift the lid on the trunk!

CHAPTER ONE

⊰⊱

The First Day

Hannah dreaded the thought of starting seventh grade—same faces, same everything as last year. A tight knot formed in her stomach as she sat near the kitchen window. Twisting a brown strand of her shoulder-length hair around a finger, she watched a caterpillar crawl across the glass. What would it be like to trade places with the caterpillar? A warm feeling tingled down her spine as she imagined herself wrapped up safely and securely in black speckled fluff.

If only there was something to look forward to, Hannah thought.

Suddenly, a bird dived straight toward Hannah, stopping just short of hitting the glass. It clung to the window frame, stretched out its neck, and made a quick meal of the helpless caterpillar. Then the bird sailed back up into the arms of the silent oak tree.

"Cool!" exclaimed her older brother. Nick had snuck up behind Hannah. "Once again, the weaker species becomes breakfast."

"Whatever," Hannah mumbled.

Nick flashed a wide smile at his sister. "Is this gonna be a great year or what?"

Of course it would be for Nick, Hannah thought. Nick, elected last spring by a landslide, was now president of the eighth grade.

"Student Council will bow to my every whim. And wait till next Friday—I'll probably catch a touchdown pass during the first game." Nick looked toward the ceiling as an imaginary football rocketed through the air. He backed up several paces, preparing to receive the ball in his arms. "And he scores!" Nick pretended to spike the ball. "Nicholas Taylor, class president and the greatest wide receiver in the history of Travis Middle School! It's got a ring to it, don't you think, Hannah Banana?"

"Earth to Nick, the universe doesn't revolve around you!" Hannah knew her brother tended to brag about himself. He had the grades and he was popular at school; she even cheered along with the crowd when he made a touchdown. The corners of her lips turned up slightly. But he still wasn't perfect, and her grades were just as good as his, even though she had to work harder at it.

Hannah and Nick both had their dad's dark brown hair, almost the exact color of a chocolate bar. But Nick's eyes were sky blue, just like their grandpa's. If you gazed deeply into her brother's eyes, you could see schemes twirling around and around. When she glanced into the mirror at her own eyes, all she could see was a deep, flat brown. That was it—no sparkle, no excitement.

Nick hummed to himself as he grabbed a bowl and spoon and sat next to her at the table. He picked up an unopened box of Crispy Flakes, turned it upside down, and shook it hard before opening it and filling his bowl to the brim. Next, he lifted the half-empty box to eye level, rotating it haphazardly as he peered inside. Flakes sprinkled onto the table and floor. "Did you find the prize yet?" Nick asked as he dug deep into the box with his free hand. More cereal spilled like confetti.

"Nicholas Cody Taylor, just look at the mess you're making!" their mother called out as she entered the kitchen. She stopped at the counter to pour a cup of coffee.

"Aw, Mom," he replied.

"I don't have time to clean up after you. Finish breakfast and get ready for school. You don't want to be late for your first day. Hannah, how are you feeling?" Mrs. Taylor kissed her daughter softly on her head, then exhaled in exasperation as Nick continued to dig through the cereal box.

"I'm fine," Hannah responded quietly, wanting to change the subject. "Oh, Mom, let him find the prize. He might need it to impress Zoe."

"Zoe?" Mrs. Taylor took a seat at the table and stirred some sweetener into her coffee.

Hannah watched Nick shift uncomfortably in his chair. "You know. Zoe McKenzie, pretty, all that blonde hair—and too much make-up," Hannah teased. "After all, Mom, how can any class president face his first day of school without a hot self-propelled Crispy Car?"

"Very funny," Nick replied. He smiled smugly as he retrieved a classic silver Corvette from the bottom of the cereal box and stuffed it into his pocket. "You never know what will come in handy."

"Come on, kids," Mrs. Taylor pleaded, "eat something." As she sipped her coffee, she picked up the morning newspaper from the table. "I don't want you to go to school on empty stomachs."

Without another word, Nick poured milk on his cereal. Satisfied, he set the carton down and attacked his food. In record time, he polished off the last bite and filled his bowl again.

"Nothing's wrong with your appetite today," Mrs. Taylor commented, skimming over the front page. "Do me a favor and try not to spill any more cereal." Nick nodded in agreement, wolfing down one spoonful after another.

Hannah watched Nick as if she were in a trance. His actions sometimes fascinated her, and apparently, he didn't mind an audience. "Maybe Student Council should set up a cereal-eating contest," Hannah giggled. "Nick will probably win first prize and be crowned King of Crispy Flakes! Another wonderfully proud moment for us to share in, Mom!"

Nick looked at Hannah. "Seriously, Hannah, even though you're a little nerdy, and I am the great Nickster, you're still my sister." He munched for a moment. "You need anything, just ask. Of course, every favor has a price," he added.

"Get real," Hannah said. "Why would I need your help?"

Just then, their mother gasped, "If we don't get moving right now, my king and queen of Travis Middle School will have their royal subjects wondering if they've moved to a new realm!"

Nick grinned and gave a satisfied burp, resulting in a look of dismay from both his mother and sister. "Hannah hasn't eaten anything," he announced.

"Squealer!" Hannah cried and pinched his arm. Nick jumped up so fast that his chair fell over with a thud. A menacing look clouded his face.

"Don't even think about it, Nicholas," Mrs. Taylor said firmly as she set the paper on the table.

"What about her?" Nick grumbled, massaging his arm.

"Hannah, quit pestering your brother. I honestly don't understand you two. Can't you see that someday you may need to rely on each other?"

Nick glared at Hannah as he reached down to pick up his chair. "That's not likely," he muttered under his breath. He shoved the chair under the table and left the room.

Mrs. Taylor gathered up the dishes and took them to the sink. "You know, Hannah, with your allergies, it's important not to skip meals." There was a sharp edge to her mother's voice.

Hannah looked blankly at her mother. "It's the first day of school—nobody but Nick can eat breakfast the first day of school." Hannah's allergies were always worse in the fall. That darn hay fever. Pollen in the air could make her wheeze, and she hated that. She must remember to take her inhaler today. *Lucky Nick,* she thought to herself. *He's always been the healthiest one in the family.*

"Hannah," her mother repeated. "I know you think I'm just being overprotective."

"Don't worry," Hannah said. "I'll grab a bagel and juice right now. I can eat on my way to school." Her mother appeared satisfied for the moment.

"Did someone say 'bagel'?" Nick shouted from the other room. "I want one too! Spread some of that straw-

Journey to the Alamo

berry stuff and cream cheese on the top, Mom. Make sure it's on really thick. I want to be able to taste it."

Hannah and her mother looked at each other and smiled. "Bottomless pit!" they sang together.

CHAPTER TWO

❧ ❧

Mr. Barrington

Travis Middle School bustled with eager students and parents as the black Suburban carrying Hannah and Nick pulled into the driveway. Teachers with bags and briefcases drifted in through a maze of traffic. Mrs. Garcia, the principal, stood at the student drop-off area, greeting everyone with a smile and a good morning.

It's still the same, Hannah thought. She watched a group of girls by the flagpole, admiring each other's new clothes. They resembled an advertisement for *Seventeen* magazine. In the middle, a very animated Zoe looked over as the Suburban came to a stop.

"Have a good day, kids," Mrs. Taylor called.

Nick opened the door and jumped out. "Bye, Mom. Hey, J.J., wait up!"

Hannah watched her brother sprint down the sidewalk toward his friend. She smiled to herself when he passed by Zoe without giving her so much as a glance. Last spring, Zoe had pretended to be her friend just so she could hang around Nick. "Maybe this year will be different," Hannah whispered.

"Honey, do you have everything you need?" her mom asked.

"I guess so, thanks. See you after school." She tossed her backpack over her shoulder, climbed out of the back seat, and swung the door closed.

When Hannah entered her first-period classroom, Jackie waved and called out, "Over here. I saved a seat for you." Jackie Montalvo, who'd moved to Austin, Texas, from California, had been Hannah's best friend for three years. She was a few inches shorter than Hannah and had straight black hair that hung halfway down her back.

Hannah took a seat near the window and noticed a man in a navy-blue suit. "Who's he?"

Jacob turned around. "Our teacher. Look at the sideburns on the guy."

"He needs some serious fashion advice," Jackie giggled. "Didn't they wear sideburns a hundred years ago?"

Hannah observed the man as he talked to Erica and Chelsea in the front row. His dark hair was pulled back and tied with what appeared to be a strip of leather. He smiled easily, and his skin had a sunburned glow.

"Good morning, class," the man said in a deep voice. "I'm your history teacher, Mr. Barrington." He removed his suit jacket and hung it over the back of a chair.

"He has really blue eyes," Jackie whispered, tapping Hannah's arm with a pencil.

Clearing his throat, Mr. Barrington turned his attention to Jackie. He had an amused expression. "Did you have something you wanted to share with the class?"

Blushing, Jackie shook her head.

"Then let's get started." Mr. Barrington pointed at two boys sitting close to the front table stacked with history books. "Would you guys give me a hand with these?" He patted the top textbook in the pile. As the books were distributed, Mr. Barrington slid his hands in his pockets and began to pace. "You're here to learn about Texas history, a subject that can be both fascinating and compelling. By the end of the first semester, you'll be experts on all the events leading up to the 1900s."

Hannah sighed and studied the faces of her friends. *No one seems fascinated with history,* she thought.

Unexpectedly, the classroom door creaked open. A janitor rolled in an old trunk on a dolly. "Where do you want this thing, Mr. B?"

"Just set it in the back," Mr. Barrington directed.

Hannah leaned to the side to get a better view of the trunk. It was huge, at least three feet long and well over two feet high, about the size of a large coffee table. Dust coated the dark brown wood. A rusty metal latch fastened the lid securely.

The janitor eased the trunk off the dolly and dropped a white rag on the top. "I still have a few boxes to cart in for the science teachers. After that, I'll give this a good cleaning."

Mr. Barrington strode to the back of the room. "Thanks, but I can handle it."

As the janitor walked out, comments bounced around the room. "Where'd you get that, Mr. Barrington?"

"Is it a pirate's chest?"

"What's in there, sir?" Jacob asked, rising to his feet. Other students followed Jacob's lead and headed to the back of the classroom.

"Come on, Hannah," Jackie coaxed.

Hannah reluctantly trailed behind the others, remaining at the outer edge of the students who gathered near the trunk and the teacher. Jackie eased her way to the middle until she stood next to Mr. Barrington.

Mr. Barrington loosened his tie and rolled up his sleeves just below his elbows. There was a small tattoo above the inside of his left wrist. "The trunk is connected to your first project. Are you sure you want to hear about it today? It's not due for weeks."

"Project," someone grumbled.

"Already?"

"Pop the top on that thing, Mr. B," Jackie insisted. "Let's see what's inside."

Mr. Barrington picked up the rag the janitor had left behind and wiped off the top of the trunk. The rag became gray as the teacher finished one side and rubbed along another. While he dusted, Hannah heard something unusual and moved closer. It was like soft shimmering cymbals. "Jacob, what's that strange noise?" she asked.

"Noise?" Jacob listened and shook his head. "I don't hear anything." Gradually, the sound of the cymbals faded.

Mr. Barrington said, "In elementary school, you learned about the battles: Gonzales, the Alamo, and San Jacinto, and the major players: Houston, Crockett, Santa Anna, Bowie, and Travis. But this year, I expect something you can really sink your teeth into. Everyone will choose an event in Texas history, research it, and become part of it."

Hannah saw a few mouths drop open. Erica said, "I don't get it. How can I become part of Texas history? It's already happened. This assignment doesn't make sense." The protests started growing louder.

Mr. Barrington's eyes twinkled as if he was keeping a secret. "This project takes creativity on your part. For some of you, it will be an exciting challenge, perhaps even an adventure." He paused, giving what he said a chance to sink in.

"An exciting challenge?" Hannah said in a hushed voice.

Mr. Barrington kneeled down beside the trunk. "Don't panic. Just think about a topic, an event in Texas history. Next Monday, we'll discuss the details."

An uneasy silence filled the air as Mr. Barrington wiggled the latch. "This thing's always been tricky to open." He walked over to his desk, removed a screwdriver from a drawer, and returned to the trunk. The circle of students grew tighter as everyone took a step forward.

Jackie giggled nervously. "Maybe there's a dead body inside."

Mr. Barrington inserted the screwdriver under the latch. "I'm afraid you're a bit too imaginative, young lady." The students laughed as he pried the latch up. The sound of soft shimmering cymbals began again. No one seemed to hear it but Hannah, and Mr. Barrington watched her as he lifted the lid. The students crowded around the trunk and peered inside.

"That's it? Only books?"

"*Texas Highways* magazines? My grandma gets those." Several students laughed at the comment.

Mr. Barrington smiled as the sound of the cymbals stopped. "These books might help you on your project. The Internet is another excellent source. Since we're short on time, why not browse through them? See if you can find a historic event that interests you."

The students started selecting books and magazines and headed back to their desks. Jackie shifted books from side to side, sorting through the contents. "Here's one with lots of pictures. Francisco Vásquez de Coronado—isn't he the guy who searches for gold?"

"That's him." Hannah slowly approached the trunk and looked at the book Jackie was holding.

"I like gold too," Jackie bubbled. "I can almost feel the connection to the past."

Hannah sighed as she glanced inside the trunk. All the magazines were gone, and the remaining books didn't even have titles. She picked up a book with a soft leather cover and walked back to her desk. *Since history is so boring, why don't I let this book choose for me?* Hannah thought. She stood the book up on its spine and let it fall open. The pages separated to reveal a picture of an old Spanish mission, the Alamo. *There's no way I'll research a battle! Like I want to become part of that.* Hannah slammed the book closed. There had to be a better choice.

She felt a presence next to her and looked up at her teacher. "You might find it will interest you more than you think," Mr. Barrington commented.

How did he know what I was thinking? Hannah wondered.

"It's almost time to leave," Jacob called out, stirring up the students.

"He's correct, class. For those of you with more questions, drop by after school. If you open your minds, you'll find that working on this project is an experience you'll never forget." Mr. Barrington smiled slyly.

The dismissal bell rang, and the class sprang into action. After placing the books and magazines back in the trunk, the bewildered students couldn't escape the classroom fast enough. None of them had known a teacher quite like Mr. Barrington.

CHAPTER THREE

Nick's Advice

After supper that evening, Hannah decided to ask Nick's advice on what to expect from the somewhat mysterious Mr. Barrington. Plopping herself down on his bed, she scanned over posters of outer space that decorated one wall and found herself momentarily airborne, soaring from planet to planet.

Nick was busy at the computer. Ignoring Hannah, he kept his back to her while he read a message from a friend.

Hannah hung over the bed and picked up an orange foam football. She sent it gliding swiftly through the air until it collided with the back of Nick's head.

"Hey, watch it," Nick protested.

"Can you stop a minute?" Hannah asked. "We need to talk."

Nick typed away, not responding.

"Come on, Nick, it won't take long—remember what you told me this morning? How you'd do anything to help me out?"

Nick stretched his fingers above the keyboard. He let out a long sigh. "That's not exactly what I meant. And right now, it's not convenient. Go ask Mom and Dad."

Hannah groaned and seized the largest pillow on the bed. Whacking her brother over the head with it brought Nick instantly to his feet. He grasped the pillow firmly and shoved Hannah backward. Losing her balance, she toppled over and landed on the bed. Nick raised the pillow over his head, ready to attack.

"Stop!" she screamed.

"What's going on up there?" their father shouted from downstairs.

"Nothing," they called out in unison. Hannah rolled over and grabbed another pillow. Swatting her brother across his shoulder resulted in returned blows.

"Time to teach you a lesson," Nick laughed wickedly.

Hannah rushed across the room to avoid her brother's assault. Nick followed close behind, cornering her near a bookcase. "I'll call Mom," Hannah said, clenching the pillow.

"Go ahead," he replied, moving forward.

Hannah swung wide in one final attempt to defend herself. Nick broke her momentum with his pillow, causing her to fall back against the bookcase. Books and football trophies plummeted to the floor. The largest trophy splintered, sending a golden plastic football rolling across the carpet.

"Oops," Hannah murmured.

"Nicholas!" their mother scolded as she stuck her head in the door. Hannah and Nick dropped their pillows at the same time.

"Did you see what she did to my trophies?" Nick asked in a not-so-innocent tone.

Mrs. Taylor glared at them. "Absolutely no more roughhousing."

Hannah and Nick stared at each other, silently debating the possibility of beginning round two.

"And I mean business," Mrs. Taylor added before she left.

Nick listened to his mother's footsteps down the hall. "Next time Mom might not be around."

Their energy zapped, Hannah bent down to help Nick pick up his things. "One question," she said, "and then I'll leave. Have you heard anything about Mr. Barrington?"

Nick pondered the question for a moment and sat back at his computer. "The guy in the suit? He's new. You're probably in for a long year. Better you than me."

Journey to the Alamo

Hannah winced.

"Just try to get on his good side. You know, charm him."

Hannah's wince turned to a grimace. "I'm not you."

Nick softened. "Why not ask that pest Jackie? She'll find out what's up with the dude. Now, get lost!"

Hannah frowned. She drifted toward the computer and watched her brother respond to his friend's message. "Mr. Barrington talked about our first project today. We're supposed to become part of Texas history. How do you do that?"

Nick typed as he answered. "There's no way. When's it due?"

"In a few weeks."

"That's a long time from now, Hannah."

"I know, but I don't want to get behind."

"Take my advice and get to know him a little better. You probably misunderstood the assignment."

"Thanks, I guess," Hannah mumbled. "Mom is picking us up late after school tomorrow. I want to work on my project."

"Fine. Go away. I'm busy."

Hannah left her brother's room. Nick was absolutely no help. She had a feeling that the more she got to know her teacher, the more confused she would be.

CHAPTER FOUR

⊰⊱

The Mysterious Trunk

The next day after school, Hannah found herself in front of room 306. "This is such a weird assignment," she whispered as she turned the knob. The door squeaked open. "Weird assignment, weird teacher, weird room."

Mr. Barrington glanced up from behind his desk as Hannah entered the room. Today, she was determined to find a topic and get more details about her assignment. She drew in a deep breath and let it out slowly. "Hi, Mr. Barrington. I'm Hannah, from first period. I have a question about the project."

Mr. Barrington placed his pen down and focused solemnly on Hannah. "I remember you. You're the one interested in the Battle of the Alamo." He adjusted his silver wire-rimmed glasses.

Hannah shook her head. "I hadn't really decided . . ."

"Mr. Barrington," announced the secretary over the intercom. "Mrs. Garcia is ready for you."

"I'll be right there," he answered. "I'm sorry, Hannah. The principal and I are meeting with a parent." Mr. Barrington pushed his chair in and started toward the door. He stopped beside Hannah as he set several papers on a student's desk. "Don't look so distressed. Everything you need is in the trunk." He straightened out the papers and slid them into a folder he was carrying. Tucking the folder under his arm, he headed for the door.

But how do I become part of history? Hannah thought.

Mr. Barrington stopped and turned back to Hannah. He removed his glasses and slid them into the pocket of his shirt. "History surrounds us, Hannah. Finding a link to the past . . . well, that's when the assignment becomes interesting. Just open the trunk."

Before Hannah could respond, Mr. Barrington was out the door. She frowned. *He did that mind-reading thing again!* Dropping her backpack beside Mr. Barrington's desk, she halfheartedly approached the back of the classroom. Then she brightened, remembering Jackie had promised to help her.

Hannah dragged a chair across the floor and sat down next to the wooden trunk. Arrows, spirals, and zigzag shapes raced around the trunk in diagonal patterns. On closer inspection, she noticed the shapes were carved and painted in yellow, orange, blue, teal, and red. The colors had probably faded with time, but the pattern was still beautiful.

A grimy assortment of discolored stickers adorned the trunk, telling a tale of its many travels: Guadalajara, Zacatecas, Béxar, Monclova, Jalapa, Mexico City. There were also diamond markings on the top, barely visible through the dust.

Dust? Hannah's eyebrows drew together. A heavy coat of dust and cobwebs, even more than yesterday, covered the surface. *I saw Mr. Barrington clean this trunk off,* Hannah thought. *There's no way spiders work that fast.*

She picked up the rag on the floor and examined both sides. It was the same rag Mr. Barrington had used, but something was wrong. There wasn't a trace of dirt on it!

Filmy cobwebs clung to the latch on the front of the trunk. Hannah swiped at the latch with the clean rag, causing it to rattle. A soft shimmering sound of cymbals began. She stopped, intrigued by the noise. The sound seemed to be coming from within the trunk. The cymbals gradually faded away. "Enough with the mysterious noises," Hannah mumbled.

More determined than ever, Hannah tried to flip up the latch. It wouldn't budge. She scraped at the rust with her fingernail and tried again. It was almost as if the trunk didn't want to be opened.

Singing softly to herself, Jackie stepped into the classroom. "You won't believe what happened after fifth period," she called out. "Jacob and Madison got in a really huge fight. I think they broke up for good this time."

Hannah wiped her hands on the rag. She was in no mood for gossip.

"What's up?" Jackie asked.

"It won't open. It's stuck."

Jackie took a fleeting glance at the trunk. "Let me try. I'll do it the same way Mr. B. did." Jackie pulled a sharp pencil out of her backpack, shoved it up under the latch, and lifted. Snap! The pencil broke in two. "That didn't work," Jackie said.

Hannah pursed her lips and forced the two halves of the pencil under the latch. The girls tried to loosen the latch together. Little by little, it started to give way until finally it jammed again. Hannah dropped her piece of the pencil to the floor. "There's nothing adventurous about this project."

"The job calls for more muscle, that's all," Jackie admitted.

"We could ask Nick."

Jackie made a face. "Are you that desperate?"

"It's already 3:50. My mom will be here soon. I'm running out of time."

Jackie ran her fingers through her hair. "I have a feeling we'll regret this."

Both girls hurried from the room and down the hall in

search of Nick. Bursting out of the front door, Jackie and Hannah scanned the school grounds. The air was heavy. A storm was brewing. Soft rays of sun slanted through the clouds, covering the campus like a pale yellow dream. Thunder rumbled, hinting the dream might turn unpleasant.

Hannah and Jackie rushed down the sidewalk and stopped under a shady tree. A group of giggling girls, including Zoe, stood behind them.

"Hannah," Zoe called out sweetly, "how was your summer?" She approached Hannah with a smile, a smile Hannah thought was a bit too cheery. Before Hannah could respond, Zoe and her friends surrounded her, forcing Jackie out of the circle.

Muttering under her breath, Jackie concentrated on her mission. Once Nick was located, she reached through the girls, grabbed Hannah by the arm, and tugged her away from the group.

"Thanks," Hannah said.

Jackie pointed at Nick, and they continued in his direction. Nick sat on a bench with J.J. and two other boys. They eyed a new Mustang that zipped through the parking lot, music blaring through the open windows.

Nick, aware Hannah and Jackie were approaching, turned away, trying his best to avoid them. Not to be put off, the girls stopped right in front of him. Hannah stood practically toe-to-toe with her brother. "I need a favor," she said.

Nick casually looked up, shading his eyes from the sun. "And?"

"And you have to help her," Jackie insisted.

"Come on, Nick," Hannah whined.

"What's in it for me?" he asked.

J.J. rose from the bench and maneuvered around to Jackie's side, his back to Nick. "Did you hear who they were talking about?" he asked quietly.

"Who?" Jackie demanded, annoyed at the interruption.

"Over there," J.J. almost whispered, his eyes darting to the girls under the tree.

Jackie exhaled in disgust. "Those clones? I don't know why you waste your time. There's nothing up here!" She tapped the side of her head several times to emphasize her point.

Embarrassed by her response, J.J. sat down, almost melting into the bench. The boys chuckled at him, Nick laughing the loudest.

Jackie glowered at Hannah's brother. "Will you help or just stare at Zoe until your mom shows up? Everyone already knows you like her." Now the boys laughed at Nick.

Caught off guard, Nick jumped to his feet and started toward the school. "Later, guys," he mumbled.

CHAPTER FIVE

The Adventure Begins

Inside Mr. Barrington's room, Nick paced around the trunk, studying its unusual markings. He touched each label as he read them aloud.

Impatient, Hannah stood with her arms crossed. "Can you open it, or not?"

A sudden flash brightened the room, followed by a clap of thunder. Outside the windows, dark clouds loomed, building upon each other. A lightning bolt streaked across the murky sky.

"Better hurry," Jackie warned, watching the weather change.

"Well?" Hannah asked.

Nick stepped away from the trunk. His brows drew together as he nodded. "Only if you promise to leave me alone for at least a week."

"That should be easy enough," Jackie said. She and Nick scowled at each other.

"And your allowance," Nick added.

"No way!" Hannah argued.

Nick stared Hannah down. "Then I leave."

Hannah gritted her teeth. "Half."

"That'll work," Nick agreed.

"Why can't you be nice to your sister?" Jackie asked.

Nick walked around to the front of the trunk. "This is nice, Jackie. Out of my way. I have work to do."

Thunder crackled, causing a chill to inch up Hannah's spine. Rain pattered lightly against the windows. Something about the storm seemed unnatural. Twin lightning bolts flashed outside the safety of the classroom as Nick's fingers touched the latch of the trunk. As he pushed up on it with both thumbs, it finally snapped open. He laughed at the girls' jumpy behavior. "Aren't you too old to be scared of storms?"

"We're not frightened," Hannah said, lifting the lid of the trunk. It popped back on its hinges and bounced. A soft shimmering sound of vibrating cymbals could be heard for just a moment. "What's that?" Jackie gasped.

"You heard it too?" Hannah asked suspiciously.

Nick shrugged. "It's probably from the air-conditioning unit. You girls get spooked way too easy."

Hannah gazed inside the trunk. The smell of mildew drifted up, bringing her back to reality. She sneezed and fanned at the stale air with her hands. "What happened to all the books and magazines?" The trunk was filled with a bizarre hodgepodge, nothing more than the sort of junk she'd seen with her mother at the flea market.

Jackie and Nick viewed the contents. "Where did Mr. B get all this stuff?" Jackie asked.

Reaching in, Hannah sorted gingerly through the collection. She moved several rolled-up papers, brown from age, to the rear of the trunk. Dog-eared journals stuck out from beneath bundles of letters tied together with strips of leather. Thick books were scattered everywhere. She picked up a faded black and white picture of a man wearing an outdated suit jacket and smoothed out the creases. "Didn't these people ever smile?" Hannah muttered. She placed the picture carefully back in the trunk and took out a tarnished compass. The glass on the top was cracked, but the arrow still pointed north. She turned it over and noticed three engraved letters on the back, "W. B. T." Without much thought, she placed it back inside.

"Aha!" Nick exclaimed as thunder crashed above the room. He grabbed a spyglass and wiped both ends with the bottom of his T-shirt. As he held it up to his right eye, he adjusted the antique device. "Hey, this really works!"

Jackie paged through a journal. "I can't read this," she blurted out. "I think it's in Spanish."

Nick turned slowly, scanning the room with the spyglass. "And outside the window, we have the storm of the century. It's turning into quite a downpour, folks." His commentary sounded like a news reporter's. "Now moving to the right, let's get a close-up on this huge, and I mean huge, hairy spider, crawling up Jackie's arm. It appears to be—"

"Eeeww!" Jackie screamed as she danced around, brushing off her sleeves.

Nick laughed, setting the spyglass down. "It's just a joke. You're way too serious."

Jackie pouted. "I don't know how Hannah puts up with you."

Nick continued to snicker as he slipped out a rolled-up paper from the trunk. It was at least two feet in length, yellowish-brown, and deteriorating from its jagged edges. He opened it on the floor and used the spyglass to hold it in place from one side and a chair on the other. Hannah stooped over to see what it was.

Nick said, "Last year, my history teacher showed us a copy of a map like this one. It's of Texas, when Texas still belonged to Mexico. Look here." Nick pointed to a spot on the map. "San Antonio is written as *san antonio de béxar*. All this old stuff must be worth a fortune."

"If it was valuable, it would be in a museum, not that musty old trunk!" Jackie corrected.

Ignoring the bickering, Hannah pulled out a well-worn jacket, fashioned from tan buckskin. She smiled at the way the fringe along the edges swayed as she held it up to get a better view. The soft leather was buttery to the touch.

Even though the jacket was a large size, Hannah tried it on. It seemed like it had been made for a giant! The bottom reached down to her knees, and her hands were lost within the sleeves. She wrinkled up her nose and sputtered, "Yuck, it smells. This must have been in there at least a hundred years! Very funny, Mr. Barrington. Is this what you mean by becoming part of history? Trying on some dead person's clothes?"

Hannah slipped the jacket off her shoulders and dropped it on the floor beside the trunk. Something else caught her eye. She pushed aside a man's wide-brimmed straw hat and slowly withdrew a wooden box, the size of one that a pair of shoes would come in. The box must have been handmade by a craftsman; it was beautiful. Its polished surface felt smooth in her hands. Most of the wood was honey-colored, but the edges were inlaid with small pieces of red. Embedded in the cover was an oval-shaped silver plate, the size of a half dollar. The image of a cannon was etched delicately into the plate. On the bottom of the box were two carved letters, "J. B." She turned it back over and started to raise the top.

BOOM! Thunder blasted directly above the classroom, and just at that moment, the lights went out.

"It's—it's like a horror movie," Nick said in a deep voice. "One of us may not live to see tomorrow."

"You're so immature," Hannah complained, pushing past her brother. She moved through the darkness toward a window. Large drops of rain pelted the glass, tapping out their own mystic rhythm.

An unusual feeling of curiosity taunted Hannah to open the box. Inside were miniature wooden soldiers, all about four inches tall. Their faces and clothing were painted on with artistic flair, and their eyes had a somber, unsettling look. Some were in uniform. She picked up one figure to study it closer. His dark blue jacket was cut short in the front, but quite long in the back, draping down almost to his knees. It didn't look like a military uniform, but he held a sword by his side. Beneath the feet of the soldier was the name *Travis.*

Jackie walked over and admired the figure Hannah held. "Someone must have carved him a long time ago," Jackie said softly.

"He looks like the picture in the trunk," Hannah said.

Hannah gently set the figure on the windowsill and

withdrew the others, one at a time. There were Santa Anna, Crockett, Bonham, Bowie, Seguín, and eight more whose names were illegible. She stood them up next to Travis in a straight row.

Nick peered over his sister's shoulder. "Nice soldiers."

The last piece cradled in Hannah's hand wasn't a figure of a man. It was a dilapidated building. Painted stones looked as if they were crumbling away from the fragile structure. Tiny holes peppered the walls, and a major portion of the roof was missing. The double doors had hinges connected to the doorframe. On the bottom were two words, *The Alamo.*

"Let me see." Nick snatched it out of her hand.

"Hey, give it back!" Hannah reached out, trying to retrieve it.

Nick dodged her attempt and positioned the Alamo in the palm of his hand. With a fingertip, he forced the doors open.

Thunder exploded like the world would end! Hannah stared in awe as lightning sprang through the sky and struck a gnarled oak tree, cracking the trunk in two. One section crashed to the ground. It landed inches from the window where they stood. A massive limb from the fallen tree reached toward them with its wet bony fingers.

"What's happening?" Jackie shrieked.

Without seeming to realize what he was doing, Nick

dropped the Alamo figurine into his pocket and yanked Hannah and Jackie away from the window.

Behind them, the shimmering sound of vibrating cymbals called from the trunk, softly at first and gradually growing louder and louder. They stood rooted to the floor in horror as a thin spiral of black glittery smoke appeared from the trunk and spun toward them. The sound of cymbals was now at a deafening roar. The smoke twisted and turned around Hannah, Nick, and Jackie until it seemed like they were positioned in the eye of a tornado.

A dizzy feeling came over Hannah. She watched helplessly as the threatening funnel spun around and around them like a top. As the smoke completely enveloped them, one last bang of thunder shook the school. The box she was holding crashed to the floor as Nick and Jackie vanished! All at once, everything turned black. Hannah was no longer in Mr. Barrington's classroom.

CHAPTER SIX

⊰⊱

The Alamo

Hannah felt the cold ground beneath her. A biting wind touched her face, daring her to open her eyes. She sat up and rubbed her throbbing head.

An old cream-colored building stood before her. Two columns twisted up each side of its arched doorway. Next to the columns were small windows. The heavy wooden double doors opened, revealing shadowy movements inside. Pieces of limestone were scattered over the earth like the building had been bombed. Hannah could barely catch her breath as she wondered where she was. *I think I need my inhaler.*

On the edge of the roof, a man surveyed the horizon through a spyglass. Behind him, a green, white, and red flag flapped proudly. Two gold stars, one above the other, decorated the white section of the flag.

To the right of the building, a sturdy line of wooden posts with sharp tips formed a tall fence. Six men aimed their rifles between spaces near the top. They hadn't noticed Hannah yet.

Wait a minute! What do I have on? Astonished, Hannah stared down at her clothes. She wore a full-length green calico dress with long billowy sleeves. The top of the dress fit snugly. Soft folds of fabric flared out from gathers at the waistline, completely covering her legs. She lifted up the bottom of her skirt a few inches. Black leather shoes with low heels had replaced her Converse sneakers. Two starched petticoats underneath her dress felt stiff and scratchy.

There was a matching jacket on the ground beside her. Shivering, she slipped on the jacket and buttoned it up to the top. She slid her hands in the pockets and discovered an inhaler. *How did this get here?* Putting it to her mouth, she depressed the top of the inhaler and took a deep breath of the spray.

She placed the inhaler in her pocket and thought back to Mr. Barrington's classroom. There had been a terrible storm. When Nick opened the doors of the miniature Alamo, a black spiral of smoke had covered them. After that, Nick and Jackie had disappeared! Where were they?

Hannah stared a second time at the crumbling fossil of a building before her. Her eyes opened wide. This was the same building as the wooden figure Nick had taken from her. This building was the Alamo, the Alamo of the past! Mr. Barrington's voice echoed in her mind, "You will choose an event in Texas history and become part of it."

Tears filled her eyes. "I don't want to be part of history! I don't want to be here at the Alamo!" She covered her face with her hands. "Mr. Barrington, what did you get me into?"

BOOM! Hannah felt the earth tremble, and something whistled through the sky. "What's that?"

A slender young woman appeared in the doorway of the Alamo church. She was wearing a dark gray dress with a white apron tied around her waist. Her light brown hair was parted in the middle and pulled back into a bun at the nape of her neck. Loose strands of hair framed her face. She rushed toward Hannah, shouting, "Why are you out here?"

Hannah was baffled. How could she explain her dilemma to anyone? Who would believe her?

The woman reached out to comfort Hannah. "Come with me to the kitchen. You're going to catch your death on this cold ground." The woman put an arm around Hannah and helped ease her to her feet. Then she guided Hannah away from the Alamo church. "What's your name?" the woman asked.

"I'm Hannah."

The woman had a kind, understanding face. One of her cheeks was smudged, and she smelled of campfire smoke. Hannah noticed her dress and apron were wrinkled and stained around the hemline. "Who are you?" Hannah sniffed.

"Susannah Dickinson."

Hannah thought she recognized the name—but from where? She had the nagging feeling that she'd heard it before.

"It's dangerous out here," Susannah said. "Why are you alone?"

"I—I don't know."

They stopped next to a building once they reached it. In front of them was a huge rectangular courtyard, and soldiers were everywhere. A few of the men wore uniforms. Others were dressed in dark baggy pants, rumpled jackets, and floppy felt hats. Silk scarves tied in droopy bows fit snugly under some shirt collars. Still others had on clothing made from buckskin. They all carried rifles or muskets and many had pistols and knives tucked into their belts.

"What's going on?" Hannah mumbled.

"We're at war! We've been under siege for twelve days now." Susannah's voice trembled. Her eyes held a weariness that came from not sleeping. "My, you act like you just walked through the front gates."

"I don't belong here."

"Many are frightened. It's especially hard on the children." Susannah gripped Hannah's hand tightly. "We have to remain strong."

Men's voices drew Hannah's attention to the high stone walls surrounding her. Some of the walls were damaged and dirt ramps led to cannons in the corners of the fort. Soldiers stood guard at the tops of buildings and walls, observing something in the distance.

Somewhat near the middle of the courtyard was an old wooden well. Nick and Jackie sat up against the well, watching the movements of the soldiers. Hannah murmured, "That's my brother over there. I'll be right back."

Susannah opened the kitchen door and stepped inside. "You hurry now, Hannah."

The beginnings of a cold misty rain drizzled down from a cloudy sky. As soon as Hannah reached the well, she knelt down beside Nick. "Where are we?" whispered Jackie, shivering. "And how did we get dressed like this? It's *so* cold!"

Nick and Jackie had on different clothes too. Nick wore a collarless shirt under a faded brown jacket. His pants had patches on the knees. Jackie was dressed in a long rust-colored skirt and a white blouse. A beige shawl hung loosely around her shoulders.

Nick's eyes shone with excitement. "I'm not sure where we are, but I think that smoky trunk is some kind of time portal."

Journey to the Alamo

"We're at the Alamo," Hannah said firmly.

Nick took in everything around him. "We're in San Antonio?"

Sharp, popping noises made them jump. "Are those fireworks?" Jackie whispered.

"It's gunfire," Hannah said nervously. "They all have guns."

"Gunfire?" Jackie gulped.

Nick studied the men on the wall. "It's the Battle of the Alamo!"

A gate made of tall planks opened up into the courtyard. A man on horseback galloped through the doorway. Hooves pounded across the ground, throwing up a cloud of dust. The man wore a wide-brimmed hat like a Mexican sombrero. A serape with colorful stripes covered his shoulders. His pant legs were frayed at the edges. He slowed the horse and dismounted in front of a building.

"Did you see that?" Jackie hissed.

"Forget him. Someone is coming this way," Nick said.

A man in a gray uniform walked away from a cannon and down the ramp. There was a knife in a sheath attached to his belt, and his knee-high black boots were scuffed. He headed toward the well with a bucket.

Nick tapped Hannah's arm and motioned for the girls to move. They scrambled around to the opposite side of the well to hide from the approaching soldier. Hannah pulled her legs in tightly toward her body, trying to disappear from sight.

The sound of the footsteps stopped. A bucket was lowered into the well and splashed when it hit the water's surface. Once the bucket was filled, the soldier turned the crank over the well, drawing it up from the bottom.

"I know you're there," the soldier called out. He unfastened the bucket and set it on the ground. Hannah shook her head and put a finger to her lips, gesturing for them to remain quiet. The soldier walked around the well and looked at them. "How long have you three been out here?"

Hannah, Nick, and Jackie slowly stood up and faced the man. No one knew how to respond to his question.

"You need to get back inside," the soldier said in a gruff tone.

Unexpectedly, an earsplitting explosion from behind the north wall caused the ground to shake and tremble. A whistling cannonball tore through the sky and grazed the upper edge of a wall. Large chunks of mortar and stones scattered across the courtyard like a handful of pebbles.

Nick hustled around the well to get a better view. At the same time, the soldier grabbed Hannah and Jackie by their arms, jerking them back from oncoming danger. The cannonball landed on the ground with a thud, and then rolled past them. Dirt fanned out from the impact.

"Let's get away from here!" Jackie screeched.

Without delay, they darted across the courtyard toward the kitchen.

As they reached the building, a pleasant aroma of spicy meat teased their senses. Someone was cooking inside. Nick took a deep breath. "What's for supper, Hannah?"

"How can you think of food at a time like this?" Hannah asked in a high-pitched voice.

The thunderous roar of another cannon followed by musket and rifle fire put an end to the questions. Hannah, Nick, and Jackie raced through the door into the protection of the building.

CHAPTER SEVEN

~☙❧~

Toribio

The kitchen door swung open with such force that it banged against the wall. Startled, Susannah looked behind her as Hannah rushed in, followed by Jackie and Nick. "Who are these two, Hannah?"

"This is my brother, Nick, and my friend, Jackie."

A short man with a bushy black mustache and caramel-colored skin moved toward them. The heels of his boots made sharp clicking noises as he stepped across the wooden floor. He had a red bandanna tied around his head. Black curls bounced out from beneath the bandanna. His hair looked too shiny, like he hadn't had time to wash it lately. "New helpers?" he asked, pronouncing each word with a crisp Spanish accent.

"Hmm, it might be a good idea to keep them busy, Toribio," Susannah agreed as she went to the fireplace.

Glancing over the girls, the man scowled at first, and then accepted the situation. "They're young, *Señora* Dickinson. *Solamente niñas.*" He focused on Nick as he wiped his hands on a dirty apron. "He looks strong enough. *Está bien.* I have work for them, plenty of work, especially since Galba has disappeared."

"Work?" Nick asked, raising an eyebrow.

Susannah lifted the lid on a cauldron and stirred the contents. The smell of stewing meat wafted up. "Hannah, where are your parents?"

Hannah bit her lip. "I—I'm not sure."

Toribio shook his head. "*Dios mío,* their parents are probably somewhere in Béxar, hiding. Perhaps they didn't make it into the fort when Santa Anna rode in with the Mexican army."

"Is that what happened?" Susannah asked.

"Uh . . . yeah, our parents aren't here," Hannah said.

Toribio smiled broadly, revealing straight white teeth. "No matter, we'll watch over you."

Hannah looked back toward the door. Could they escape?

It was too late. Toribio had already taken Jackie by the arm, leading her to the back of the kitchen. "*Mija,* I have some nice *cebollas* for you to chop. Your friend can help you."

"*Cebollas?*" Jackie winced, gaping at a pile of onions on a table.

Susannah replaced the lid on the cauldron. "I'll have to speak with Colonel Travis about these three, but for now, they can stay put."

Toribio handed Jackie and Hannah long knives, and then he turned to Nick. "I need water, *mijo.* The bucket is at the end of the table. Do you know where the well is?"

Nick shoved his hands in his pockets and stared at the fireplace. Toribio frowned. His heels clicked back across the floor. The man picked up a bucket and held it out to Nick. "We have over two hundred people to feed, and I need water, *entiendes?*"

Hannah gave Nick an encouraging nudge. "Okay, okay, I'll be right back," Nick muttered. He took the bucket and headed to the door.

"I should check on my daughter," Mrs. Dickinson explained. "I left her with Mrs. Esparza. When I return, we'll have that visit with the colonel."

Hannah heard the popping of rifle fire when Nick and Susannah left the kitchen. Inside was safer than outside. She hoped Nick would hurry back. She also made up her mind to go along with whatever was happening, for now. What choice did they have?

Jackie's forehead wrinkled. "This knife is dirty." She held it up so Toribio could see the evidence.

He shrugged, took the knife, and wiped it off on his apron. "Here, *mija.*" He handed her the knife and went back to work.

Hannah stared at Jackie. "Hasn't anyone told him about antibacterial dish soap?"

"Did you see the dirt under his fingernails?" Jackie asked.

Hannah cut off the end of an onion. "We have a much bigger problem. How do we get home?"

The door creaked open as a man entered. A wide-brimmed hat was pulled down low on his head and his gaze swept the floor. He stopped quietly at the edge of the table. He glanced nervously from Hannah to Jackie as he shifted his weight from side to side. "Excuse me, miss," he said softly. "I come to fetch Mister Travis's lunch."

Hannah set her knife down. "What do we give him, Jackie?"

With the blade of her knife, Jackie gathered the chunks of onion into a pile. "I can make a good ham and cheese sandwich. Does he want it with or without mayo?"

The man looked confused. "I don't know nothin' 'bout mayo. Whatever you have cookin' in that kettle yonder is fine."

"Toribio!" Jackie shouted. "We have one order to go

for Mr. Travis! And don't forget to hold the mayo!"

Toribio approached Jackie as he wiped his hands on his apron. "What is this mayo you are talking about?"

"Oh, oh," Jackie whispered.

"It's like a seasoning," Hannah explained. "Something our mothers use."

Toribio glanced at Hannah as he picked up a plate. "I have never heard of mayo," he said. "Where does it grow?"

"Toribio," Jackie said in a soft voice. "The guy is waiting."

"Of course," Toribio agreed. "*Señor* Travis hasn't eaten all day." Toribio hurried over to the fireplace. He dished up a generous portion of steaming meat from a smaller pot sitting away from the fire, covered the plate with a cloth, and handed it to the man. "Here it is, Joe."

"Thank you," Joe said without smiling as he turned to leave.

"Who is he?" Hannah whispered as Joe left the kitchen.

Toribio examined the chunks of onion on the table. "*Mijitas,* these need to be much smaller."

Jackie rolled her eyes and pouted.

"Toribio?" Hannah pressed for an answer.

"Oh, that man? He's *Señor* Travis's slave." Toribio took Jackie's knife and chopped the large sections of onion in front of her into smaller pieces. "Like this, *entiendes?*"

"I know how to do it," Jackie griped.

"A slave?" Hannah gulped.

"Haven't you seen him before?" He handed the knife back to Jackie. "*Señor* Travis keeps him very busy."

"Slavery is—is so unfair," Jackie protested. "How can you own another person?"

Toribio shook his head. "I don't understand it either. In Mexico, slavery had almost disappeared—until the *norte americanos* came to live here. Some, like Travis, brought slaves with them."

Hannah set her knife down and pushed her hair behind her ears. "Will he fight beside Travis?"

Toribio shrugged. "If he belongs to *Señor* Travis, he must know how to handle a weapon."

By the time Nick returned with the water, Toribio was at another table cutting up a hindquarter of beef with a cleaver. Hannah and Jackie had tears streaming down their faces. Hannah wiped off the tears on her sleeve and sliced open another onion.

Nick's eyes narrowed. He set the bucket down and confronted Toribio. "What did you do to my sister?"

Bringing the cleaver down hard, Toribio separated a chunk of meat from a long bone. He looked curiously at Nick. "Do? I've been telling them all about a village I once lived in. It was a most beautiful land with—"

"Why are they crying?" Nick said accusingly.

Toribio smiled. "*Las cebollas.*"

"*Cebollas?*" Nick repeated. Judging from his blank expression, he had no idea what *cebollas* were.

"It's the onions," Hannah whimpered. "They're really strong."

Jackie giggled through the tears. "How sweet! Nick is worried about us, Hannah."

"Shut up, Jackie." Nick brooded as the girls laughed at his sudden urge to defend them.

Toribio emptied the water into the cauldron over the fireplace. The liquid sizzled as it reached the meat at the bottom. Steam rose from the top while he stirred the stew. He held out the bucket to Nick again. "I need more, *mijo.*"

"Fine." Nick grabbed the bucket, muttered under his breath, and stomped out of the kitchen.

As he left, another young man entered. He was a few years older than Nick. There was a gaping hole in one knee of his pants. His smile practically reached his ears when he noticed the girls in the kitchen. Quickly, he attempted to smooth down his jet-black hair.

"Galba, where have you been?" Toribio scolded. The cleaver he wielded came down with such force it sliced through the meat like paper and bit into the wood of the table.

Galba tensed up and his smile faded. "They asked me to brush down a horse. I told 'em you'd miss me."

"*Sí, sí,* I am certain you told them a story, but what story?"

Journey to the Alamo

Galba approached Toribio with caution. After all, the man was cutting up a hindquarter like it was kindling. Galba spoke to the cook in such a low voice that the girls couldn't overhear. Toribio's eyes widened with interest, and then he nodded.

"What are they talking about?" Hannah whispered to Jackie.

"I don't know, but Galba—is that what he called him— keeps looking at you."

Hannah blushed. "He's making me nervous."

After hoisting up a lumpy cloth bag from the floor, Toribio walked over to the table where the girls worked. Galba tagged along behind him. Hannah and Jackie had just finished the onions. Their tears had stopped, but their eyes remained red.

Toribio plopped the bag down on the table, cleared his throat, and faced the girls. "*Señoritas,* I would like to present *Señor* Galba Fuqua from Gonzales."

Galba nodded politely. "Howdy."

"Howdy?" Jackie giggled. "Do people from Gonzales actually say howdy?"

Toribio stared at Jackie and shook his head, quieting her giggles. "And these *señoritas* are Hannah and Jackie. There, I have done what you asked, Galba." Toribio opened the bag and spilled the contents on the table. Potatoes rolled everywhere. "Now that you are all acquainted, start peeling." His heels clicked back across the floor.

"What does he have on the bottom of those boots?" Jackie asked.

Hannah shrugged. "Galba, do you and Toribio always work in the kitchen?"

"Nope, we're just helping out. Most times we're standing guard at the wall. Toribio, he's a jack-of-all-trades. He knows everything about soldiering."

"Sounds like you look up to him," Hannah said.

Galba nodded. "I seen him in action. He's a deadly shot."

Hannah picked up a potato and tried to figure out the best way to peel it with the large knife she was holding. Her mother did most of the cooking at home, so this task was a puzzle.

Galba removed a dagger from a sheath on his belt and handed it to Hannah. "This one's smaller. It'll be easier for you to handle."

Hannah lowered her eyes and smiled. "Thanks."

CHAPTER EIGHT

David Crockett

Hannah sighed, relaxing at a table across from Nick. Instead of chairs, they sat on long benches. "I never want to see another onion or potato for the rest of my life," she muttered.

Jackie set three plates of beef stew down on the table. "My fingers still smell like onions."

Nick's disposition seemed to improve with the sight of food before him. Toribio had taken Galba on an errand, so the three of them were finally alone.

"What will happen to us when the battle begins?" Hannah asked. Jackie's eyes grew wide.

"This is too cool." Nick gobbled up the stew. "We're going to be eyewitnesses to the Battle of the Alamo! That means it's March, 1836. Why didn't I have a history teacher like Mr. Barrington last year?"

"Don't you get it?" Jackie snapped. "We're in a life-threatening situation!"

"Lighten up, Jackie," Nick said.

Hannah blew lightly on a spoonful of stew. "We're in this together. We should try to get along."

Nick coughed, and then cleared his throat. He glanced at Jackie sitting next to him. They glowered at each other. Jackie scooted a few inches away from Nick. She said, "Didn't that lady say we were supposed to meet with Colonel Travis? It's a bad idea. What will we tell him?"

"That lady is Susannah Dickinson," Hannah said.

Jackie watched the steam rise up from her plate. "I remember reading about her in a library book. She survives the battle."

"I knew her name sounded familiar," Hannah said.

"She's the one who tells Sam Houston what happened at the Alamo," Nick mumbled with a full mouth. "He's the commander of the Texas army."

Hannah pushed some stew around on her plate. "You sure remember a lot from your history class."

Nick swallowed another spoonful. "The battle's pretty gruesome, a bloody mess."

Hannah cringed. Suddenly the food didn't appeal to her.

"We better be careful with the timeline," Nick said. "We might not get home if we change the past. Before Susannah comes back, we better be gone."

The door opened, and Toribio led a line of soldiers into the kitchen. Their clothes were rumpled, and some of the men had dark circles under their eyes as if they hadn't slept in days.

Hannah bent her head to take a bite and noticed the last soldier as he passed by. The man had on a peculiar hat made out of fur with a ringed tail in the back. His long hair hung past his collar. Fringe dangled off the back of his sleeves and the bottom of his tan buckskin jacket. His face was a blur, but there was something familiar about his stride. Hannah turned around to get a second look. All she could see was a tall man's back.

Toribio served each soldier a dish of stew. Some took their food outside while others sat at the tables, talking in low voices. Hannah shook her head and faced the table again.

"This food is really good," Jackie admitted. "I hope there's enough for everyone."

"Did I hear you correctly?" boomed a deep voice with a southern drawl. "There's nothin' more delicious than Toribio's cookin'!" The soldier in the buckskin jacket sat down next to Hannah and put his plate on the table.

Nick and Jackie gawked at the man. "Davy Crockett," Nick whispered reverently.

The man chuckled, "I guess ever'one knows who I am, even in Texas."

Excited to meet a true Texas legend, Hannah turned to the man next to her. "Mr. Barrington!" she called out in surprise. In spite of his rugged clothing and loose hair, he looked exactly like her history teacher. There was also a spark in his eyes that Hannah recognized, and she was anxious to get this dilemma resolved. "You came to our rescue!"

"I don't know who Mr. Barrington is, sweetheart. I'm David Crockett. I'll be obliged to help you any way I can. Now, why don't you tell me your names?"

Hannah was confused. Mr. Barrington knew her name. She looked at Nick, but he shrugged as he scraped up the last of his meal. "I'm Hannah, and this is Nick and Jackie."

The man savored a mouthful of stew. "Mmmm, these are mighty fine vittles."

"Mr. Crockett?" Nick said.

The man grinned. "Don't need no misters with me. Just call me David like ever'body else, and we'll git along fine."

"Did you bring Betsy?" Nick asked.

"I left Ole Betsy at home with my son. But I have another I haven't named yet. In fact, she's settin' behind me." He turned and pointed to the door. "Go fetch her so you can git a better look."

Nick jumped up and bounded to the corner. He had already forgotten to ask for a second serving of stew.

Jackie watched Nick hurry toward the door. "I don't see anyone sitting in the corner."

"Who's Betsy?" Hannah asked.

David smiled. "Betsy's my younger sister. I named two of my rifles for her, Ole Betsy and Pretty Betsy. Ole Betsy and me've been through many tangles together."

Nick carried a rifle back to the table, admiring the beautiful wooden stock. It looked longer and heavier than modern hunting rifles, and the barrel was an octagonal shape instead of round.

"Handle her gently, son," David said.

When Nick set the rifle down, it took up almost the entire length of the table. David finished the last of his meal. "If it weren't for those pesky *soldados* outside that wall, Nick, we'd go huntin' right now." He rose to his feet, almost touching the ceiling with his head. "Hear the white-tail 'round Béxar are good eatin'." David took his empty plate and carried it back to Toribio.

Hannah thought carefully about the man's voice. He didn't sound anything like Mr. Barrington. Even Nick and Jackie were drawn to his words. Maybe he really was David Crockett. Not quite convinced, she stared at him again.

"Hannah, he's not your teacher," Nick said in a low voice.

"I'm not so sure," Hannah murmured.

"He's Crockett," Nick disagreed. "Take another look at his rifle."

"And those clothes," Jackie whispered. "That's exactly how I'd picture him dressed."

"But he looks like Mr. Barrington," Hannah insisted.

Jackie leaned forward. "I don't see it. This guy is taller and his hair, I think it's lighter."

Nick pushed his plate to the side. "Get a grip, Hannah. Why would he lie about who he is?"

Hannah sighed. "He does have a weird accent."

"Shhh, he's coming back," Jackie said. "And he calls himself David, not Davy."

"All right, all right. Have it your way. He's David Crockett," Hannah admitted grudgingly.

David strolled back to the table. "*Gracias* for the tasty vittles, Toribio."

The cook smiled. "*De nada, Señor* Crockett."

David looked thoughtfully at the three still seated. "Why don't y'all come with me to the barracks? I'm meetin' a man there who once lived in Scotland. I play my fiddle, and he plays the bagpipes."

Hannah twisted a strand of hair around her finger. "Good idea." This would give them the chance they needed to avoid Susannah Dickinson, and at the same time she could discover who this man really was, Mr. Barrington or David Crockett.

CHAPTER NINE

~Я Ӗ~

The Mexican Army

"Hand me my rifle," David said. Nick gave the gun one last look before he placed it in the seasoned frontiersman's hands. Then they followed David out into the courtyard.

The afternoon had darkened, quickly turning into nighttime. A gusting north wind whipped across the courtyard, snapping the lower edge of Hannah's dress around her ankles. Hannah shivered, and Jackie pulled her shawl tighter around her arms. Nick seemed totally unaware of the weather. Walking next to David Crockett and chatting like old friends, he was too excited to feel any drop in temperature.

David paused outside the kitchen and pointed to the

fence line Hannah had noticed when she first appeared on the ground before the Alamo church. David said, "The palisade is one of the weakest spots in the walls. Since me and my friends are crack shots, Travis posted us there. The *soldados* don't dare venture into the sights of our rifles."

As they crossed the courtyard toward the barracks, a man shouted, "Fire!"

BOOM! An explosion shook the ground like an earthquake. Startled, Hannah looked up at a dirt ramp. A menacing cloud of black smoke spouted from the mouth of a cannon. Cheers arose from the Alamo defenders at the tops of the walls.

"My ears are ringing!" Jackie shouted over a second blast from another cannon.

"Better get used to it," David suggested. "The cannon fire hasn't let up since I got here. It's a shame we're short on cannonballs. Every time one flies over the walls, we haul it up to one of our cannons and send it lickety-split right back to the Mexicans. We even use horseshoes and cut-up chains in place of cannonballs."

"Can we look over the wall?" Nick asked eagerly.

"I reckon a gander wouldn't hurt." David pointed to the southwest corner of the courtyard. "Our eighteen-pounder sits up there."

"Eighteen pounds of what?" Hannah asked.

Jackie shrugged.

"He's talking about the size of a cannon," Nick said.

"Oh," the girls replied in unison.

They followed David toward the dirt ramp that led up to a cannon tended by four soldiers. One soldier swabbed out the inside of the wide barrel. Another dipped water from a bucket and poured it over the cannon to cool it down.

"Why are they in gray uniforms?" Jackie asked.

David slowed his pace. "They're the New Orleans Greys. They come all the way from Louisiana for the cause."

"They're a long way from home," Hannah commented softly. "Just like us."

When they reached the top of the ramp, David patted one of the soldiers on his back. "How you boys doin'?"

"Best we can," the man answered. He pointed to a line of Mexican cannons in the distance. "They're too far to hit, but we're aiming to keep them from moving any closer." David nodded in agreement.

Another soldier handed Hannah a spyglass. "Here, take a look." It was similar to the one Nick had found in Mr. Barrington's trunk.

Hannah held the spyglass up to her eye. Out on the prairie, enemy soldiers paraded on horseback: the Mexican cavalry. They carried long lances with red flags festooned from the tops. Farther out, white peaks of tents covered the land. Campfires dotted the ground with golden hues in front of the small low tents. Soldiers in white pants and navy jackets gathered about the fires. As far as Hannah could see, the fort was completely surrounded. "There must be hundreds of soldiers out there."

"Not hundreds, Hannah, there's thousands," David corrected in a low voice.

"Thousands?" Jackie squeaked.

Hannah glanced back at the soldiers scattered throughout the courtyard. How could so few men stand up against thousands?

"Artillery fire from the enemy eases up after sunset," David said. "When a breeze blows in just so, you can even smell their cooking fires."

Nick pointed to a blood-red pennant over a Spanish-styled building. "Whose flag is that?"

A soldier set his bucket down. "Santa Anna had them raise that flag to the top of the San Fernando Cathedral as a warnin'. It's a flag of no quarter. It means no prisoners will be taken when the battle has ended. Anyone alive will be uh, I guess you could say . . . executed."

"I don't understand," Jackie said. "No prisoners?"

David's smile hardened to a thin line. "Santa Anna fancies himself emperor of Mexico. He's fixin' to punish us rebels in Texas for tryin' to make our own government. Seems he'll do anything to scare people into packin' up and skedaddlin' like jack rabbits back to the United States."

"Why did so many people move here from the United States?" Hannah asked.

"Mexico welcomed homesteaders for a spell. Many Americans settled down right comfortable here in Texas. After a few years, things started to change. The Mexican government wanted to regulate trade and stop United States immigrants from movin' in. That's what our flag flyin' above the Alamo church means, a statement to Mexico that we're demandin' our rights."

"I saw it," Hannah reflected, "the flag with the two gold stars in the center."

"At first, the *tejanos* and the Texians were hopin' they could somehow convince the government to return to the Constitution of 1824. They took the eagle off the Mexican flag and put on two gold stars to stand for our state of *coahuila y tejas*. It's our way of sayin' don't forget us. But not everyone in Texas feels the same way. There's those that want to remain part of Mexico. We're aimin' for independence." David's eyes narrowed as he scratched the unshaven whiskers on the side of his face. "We have some serious business to tend to with them fellers out there."

For a moment, everyone watched the movements of the Mexican army. Hannah felt overwhelmed by the sheer number of enemy soldiers. *What if we're still here when the battle begins?*

"Well, well," David said, gazing back into the courtyard.

"The men already have two campfires goin'. Follow me."

The girls had a difficult time keeping up with David's long strides down the ramp. They didn't stop until they reached an area right in front of the barracks on the east side of the courtyard. A crowd of men had gathered, and Hannah noticed their spirits lifting when Crockett joined them. David laughed and joked as he shook hands with a few of the men. "I need to fetch my fiddle inside. I'll be back in two shakes of a tail."

Nick sat next to Hannah and Jackie on a log by the smaller fire that was the furthest from the defenders. Thoughts of war were pushed aside. The warmth of the fire as well as the jovial mood of the men let everyone enjoy the camaraderie, at least for a short while.

"My feet hurt! These boots are too tight," Jackie complained as she massaged her toes through the stiff leather.

Nick crossed his leg and lifted up his foot high enough so Jackie could see the sole of a very old shoe. "You don't know what pain is until you've tried these on." There was a gaping hole on the bottom of his shoe. Both girls giggled.

Nick suddenly looked serious as he asked, "Do either of you know what's about to happen?"

"I don't remember all the details of the battle," Hannah confessed.

Jackie looked around. "Hurry before someone overhears."

Nick moved closer to Hannah. "It won't be long before the battle begins. Two of the main heroes you should recall besides Crockett are William Barret Travis and James Bowie. They all died fighting for Texas."

"And Juan Seguín?" Hannah asked. "Wasn't he here?"

"He survived because Travis sent him out with a message to Houston. But some of his men remained behind. Before Seguín could return, the battle was over. It takes days to get anywhere on horseback."

"Remember the Alamo," Jackie whispered.

Hannah considered what was about to take place. These wonderfully alive people would write Texas's history with their own blood. Her heart sank. Was this the lesson Mr. Barrington wanted her to learn?

The good-natured banter of the soldiers was interrupted by a lonesome wailing melody emerging from the barracks. John McGregor popped out of the door, playing his bagpipes. The tune was slow and mournful, and soon all conversation ended as the entire group seemed to become lost in lingering thoughts of home or someone left behind. The wistful mood of the music held everyone's attention.

Once McGregor finished, Hannah could see tears in the eyes of a few of the soldiers. She thought, *These brave men will never see home or loved ones again. They're willing to die for the freedom of Texas.*

Bright and cheery fiddle music lifted over the grounds

as David took his place next to McGregor. A red fox tail hung from his fiddle bow, different from the one on his hat. It bobbed back and forth while he played a spirited song.

John joined in on the bagpipes, and the audience clapped and sang in time to the music. Some began to dance, locking arms while stepping lightly over the ground. One young soldier pulled Jackie to her feet, enticing her to dance with him. He twirled her around to the lively beat.

Hannah watched Jackie trying to figure out the dance steps. "That boy isn't old enough to be fighting in any war."

"I think whoever could be spared from their farm or knew how to handle a gun joined the fight," Nick explained. "They didn't want to give up their land or way of life. Would you?"

"I guess not. We have it so easy. If it weren't for these people, things might be very different."

Nick stared at Hannah. His enthusiasm for the sights and sounds of the Alamo had dwindled. "Something else I remember from history class—how short the battle was, about an hour and a half."

Hannah shuddered. "That's the length of a movie." An eerie sensation prickled on the back of her neck. "What about us? Do you think Mr. Barrington—David Crockett— will get us away from here in time?"

"Don't count on him, Hannah. Crockett dies here, on these grounds."

Hannah studied David's profile as his bow glided across the strings of the fiddle. Almost everything about him was the same as Mr. Barrington except for his clothes and southern drawl.

Nick mumbled, "It won't be long before thousands of Mexican soldiers find a way over those walls."

The music continued to weave around them in a complicated pattern. Hannah knew exactly what Nick was thinking. *How will we ever get home?*

CHAPTER TEN

Boys from Gonzales

A smitten young man escorted Jackie back to the fire. She giggled as she sat down next to Hannah. Her cheeks were flushed from the dance, and her eyes sparkled. "Hannah, this is Will King from Gonzales."

Will removed his hat and attempted to straighten out his tousled sandy-blond hair. It stuck out in different directions as if it had been styled in modern times. Freckles were scattered lightly over his cheeks and nose, and there was something about his eyes that reminded Hannah of Nick, that same self-confidence.

Will politely extended his hand. "Howdy, Hannah. Pleasure to meet you." He gave Hannah a firm handshake. His hand was rough and calloused from hard work.

Hannah snuck a look at Jackie, and they both giggled. Nick cleared his throat as a reminder to the girls he was still there. "Oh, and this is Hannah's brother, Nick," Jackie chirped.

Will grinned and shook hands with Nick. "I hope I wasn't out of line asking Jackie for a dance."

Nick and Jackie gave each other a distasteful glare as Hannah smothered a laugh. "Her?" Nick grumbled. "Dance with both of them. The farther away, the better."

Will spun around and put his fingers to his lips, producing a piercing whistle that echoed through the courtyard. In response, Galba sauntered through the crowd of defenders.

Will waved his arm in the air and called out, "Over here, Galba! We have dance partners!"

Galba quickened his pace until he stood beside Hannah. Before she had a chance to consent, Galba took her hand, pulled her away from the campfire, and swung her around the courtyard to a Tennessee tune.

At first, Hannah watched her feet as she learned the steps. Before long, she felt comfortable with the movements and started to follow the music. "Are you and Will friends?" Hannah asked as another melody began.

"Me an' Will are as close as brothers can be without sharin' blood. My Uncle Ben is married to his sister. We're family to the bone." Galba stepped back and twirled Hannah in a circle. Her skirt fanned out like petals on a flower, but her feet seemed to go in opposite directions.

"Turning's not that easy," Hannah laughed, struggling to remain upright.

"Try it again?" Galba asked.

Hannah nodded eagerly. Galba stepped back and twirled her another time. Hannah held her breath and balanced on her toes. She watched the courtyard pass by as she spun around.

"Much better," Galba complimented.

Hannah smiled and applauded for the musicians as the tune ended. "I think I'm ready for a break."

As they walked back toward the barracks, Hannah noticed Nick talking to a different young man. "Do you know him?"

"Johnny Gaston," Galba said, "another friend of mine."

"Aren't the three of you kind of young to be here?" Hannah blurted out before she had a chance to stop herself. She didn't want to appear too surprised by what everyone else saw as normal.

"Old enough, I reckon," Galba replied calmly. "Johnny's seventeen, Will's fifteen, and I'm sixteen."

Once they reached the fire, Galba rolled over a short log to act as a bench. Hannah sat down and held out her hands to warm them.

Journey to the Alamo

"This is my sister, Hannah," Nick said to Johnny. She smiled shyly at Johnny. He nodded and touched the wide brim of his brown felt hat. Dark wavy hair hung loose from beneath his hat and curled up at the ends. Even though his face was shadowed, his hazel eyes picked up the golden light of the flames as he peered at Hannah. There was a bleak, almost haunted look reflected in them.

He doesn't want to be here, Hannah thought, suddenly feeling sad as well.

"When did you get here?" Nick asked.

Johnny set an ancient musket to the side of him. "Rode in a few days ago."

Hannah studied Johnny's old musket. David's rifle looked newer and well cared for. Johnny's was much different. The wooden stock of the musket had lost its shine from being handled by too many people, possibly different owners. Hannah wondered if the musket even worked properly. "How did you get past all those Mexican soldiers surrounding the fort?" she asked.

"Weren't easy," Johnny said. "We come in late at night. Used darkness for cover." Johnny watched Galba sit down next to Hannah. "Will and Galba here think this is one grand adventure."

Galba flinched and shook his head. "You worry too much, Johnny."

The flames flickered as a large piece of kindling split in

half, crackling and popping. Johnny concentrated on the fire. "I've been posted up on the wall. I seen 'em. More enemy soldiers than I can count, and they just keep comin'. If help don't arrive soon . . ." His voice quieted to almost a whisper. "It ain't like before."

"Before?" Nick asked, crossing his leg. He picked up a rock and started scraping dried mud off the bottom of his shoe.

Johnny leaned forward, resting his elbows on his knees. "When the Mexican soldiers come to Gonzales in late September, I was a lookout on the Guadalupe River. About a hundred dragoons rode in. They was sent to fetch our only cannon."

Galba turned to Hannah. "A few years back, they gave us the cannon for protection from the Comanche."

Comanche? Hannah shuddered and rubbed her arms to warm them. "What's a dragoon?" She thought how much the word sounded like *dragon,* but she knew dragons were only mythical creatures.

Johnny glanced sideways at her, and Hannah could see his jaw tighten. "Mexican cavalry, soldiers on horseback. They're experts at what they do, well trained and well armed."

"What happened?" Nick asked.

Johnny reached down, put his hand on his musket, and then released it. "We gave 'em a taste of our Texian mettle. Stood our ground and sent 'em back to Béxar with their tails betwixt their legs without the cannon. Not one of ours was killed." He lowered his voice again. "This is different."

"How?" Hannah asked nervously, thinking how close to the truth Johnny was.

He took in a deep breath and slowly exhaled. "In Gonzales, reinforcements from surroundin' areas arrived within a matter of hours. I've been here for days. Not even Fannin's troops have showed up from Fort Defiance in Goliad. It's the closest military compound to Béxar. Our best hope."

Galba groaned as he stood up. "Don't scare her, Johnny." He turned away from the group and watched the musicians.

"No sense sugar-coatin' it," Johnny scoffed. "We all know what's out there, Galba."

Hannah listened for a moment to the men's voices in the crowd as conversations blended into the music. The words weren't clear, but the tone was bold, some laughter a little too loud. The tension was heavy. Hannah swallowed. Galba wasn't sure what they were up against, but Johnny knew.

"Why do you stay, Johnny?" Nick asked.

Johnny's eyes darted along the walls of the fort, then to the fire, and back to the walls again. He rubbed his hands together, warming them, and cracked his knuckles. He smiled for the first time. "Ever been to Gonzales?"

Nick shook his head and stretched out his arms.

"My family has a cabin near the river. It's good land. We didn't have nothin' like it before we come to Texas. As for my friends, we hunt and fish together. Catfish practically beggin' to be tossed in the fryin' pan. Ever'one there sticks together, helps each other out. They're good people." His voice softened. "Worth fightin' for."

Johnny grabbed his musket and got to his feet. He was tall and lanky, much taller than his friends were. He picked up a piece of split wood and added it to the fire. It sent sparks climbing up into the chilly air. "Come on, Galba. We're expected to keep watch—orders." His voice trailed off as if he was talking only to himself. "Promised Ma I'd come home safely."

Galba took a few steps and stopped. "Hannah, will you promise me a dance another night?"

Looking down, Hannah smoothed out her skirt. "Okay," she replied.

Grinning, Galba reluctantly followed Johnny toward the wall. When he reached the middle of the courtyard, he turned back and called out, "See you tomorrow, Hannah."

Hannah waved to her new friends as they walked away. Her cheeks held a rosy glow.

"Don't get too attached, Hannah," Nick warned.

"What do you mean?"

"These guys aren't from the neighborhood. They're never going home."

Hannah watched Galba and Johnny take their places on the wall. As they moved farther away, they seemed to blur into nothingness against the night sky. "We should warn them!" she gasped.

"What can we say?"

Hannah bit her lip. She didn't have an answer to that question. All she knew was life wasn't fair in 1836.

As if on cue, the music changed to a slow, melancholy song. Jackie and Will, ready for a break, approached the fire. "Why the long face?" Jackie asked, sitting down next to Hannah. Jackie worked at retying the ends of her shawl to help hold it in place.

Hannah glanced at Will, standing by the fire. "It's something Nick said," Hannah whispered.

"Hmph, just like him to spoil your fun," Jackie commented as she tightened the knot in her shawl.

"You don't understand," Hannah explained. "He just reminded me of some important facts about—"

"Where's Galba?" Will interrupted.

Nick pointed to the west wall. "He's up there with Johnny."

Will paused while the audience clapped for the musicians. "Johnny's so serious about this revolution. I swear, sometimes he's got the eyes of an old man. Talks about reasons things happen and such. Sees more than what's in front of him." Will hooked his thumbs in his pockets and stared at the wall. "Me and Galba, well, we jest want a chance to shoot our muskets and send Santy Anny clean back to Mexico City."

"Gutsy words," Jackie crooned with admiration.

"Most anything's better than workin' on the farm," Will chuckled.

Hannah looked up at the largest star in the inky sky. A lump formed in her throat as she closed her eyes and made a silent wish, something she hadn't done in years. She wished the three boys from Gonzales would be sent out as messengers before the battle began.

Will held out his hand. "Would you honor me with one last dance, Jackie?"

Jackie jumped up excitedly and took his hand. She seemed to have no thoughts of the upcoming battle; she was savoring this night. Will led Jackie into the crowd.

One last dance? Guilt welled up in Hannah as she moved to sit beside Nick.

Nick noticed his sister's grim expression. "You can't save them, Hannah. History has already been written. The only unknown factor is the part we play."

Unexpectedly, Hannah leaned up against her brother for comfort. "I want to go home, Nick."

CHAPTER ELEVEN

❦

The Line in the Sand

Hannah and Nick watched Susannah Dickinson gather her skirts about her and hurry through the courtyard. Susannah worked her way through the defenders, who were still enjoying the music and talking to each other.

"Susannah," David called out. He stopped playing for a moment, but McGregor continued. "Who you looking for?"

"I'm worried about some children," Susannah replied. As Jackie danced by, Susannah took her arm. They both walked toward the campfire.

"Thanks for the dance, Will!" Jackie shouted, trying her best not to trip over her skirt, which had tangled around her legs.

Nick tapped Hannah's arm. "Here comes Susannah."

"She's only trying to help us, Nick."

"I don't think she can. Our best chance out of here is to reconnect somehow with the future."

Hannah picked up a stick and scratched in the dirt. The scratches took shape and formed the image of a crude box. "A connection like Mr. Barrington's trunk?"

A spark of inspiration shone in Nick's eyes. "That's it, Hannah! It must've come here with us. If we find the trunk, we go home."

"I only saw tables in the kitchen," Hannah reflected. "It wasn't in there."

"Since Crockett had his violin in the barracks . . ." Nick didn't have a chance to finish because Susannah and Jackie stood before them. Jackie sat down on a log next to Hannah.

"I thought you'd still be in the kitchen," Susannah said. "No matter. It's time we found Colonel Travis."

"Let them stay here for a while, Susannah," drawled a masculine voice behind them. "Travis will be here shortly. He wants the men to join him in the courtyard."

Susannah turned her attention to a man lying on a cot behind her. His skin was pale, almost a yellowish-gray color. He motioned for two soldiers to carry him closer to the fire. As soon as they set the cot down, he pushed himself up and rested on his elbow. Holding a handkerchief up to his mouth, he coughed into it. The man had difficulty breathing as well as getting comfortable on the low narrow bed. Hannah hadn't noticed him before. Had he been there all along?

"Colonel Bowie," Susannah said, "it's not safe out here for children."

Bowie struggled to draw in a deep breath. "It's hard for them to be cooped up in a building all day. Besides, I rather like seeing these young ladies dance and enjoy themselves. Reminds me of another time."

Bending over him, Susannah pulled out a handkerchief from an apron pocket and dabbed at the perspiration covering his face.

"The cannon fire has let up for the night," Bowie explained. "After Travis talks to the men, he'll get to these young'uns. You have my word on it."

"If you insist," Susannah said with a sympathetic tone.

Bowie coughed again and gave Hannah and Jackie a quick wink. Susannah gently touched Bowie's forehead. "You still have fever."

"Night air will cool me down," he said. "I'll be fine."

Susannah's expression showed disbelief in his words. Bowie looked like he should be resting in a hospital, not outdoors. She said, "This young man is Nick, and these two are Hannah and Jackie."

Bowie nodded as he focused on Hannah. "The three of you stay close now," he said.

With a sigh of acceptance, Susannah nervously straightened out the folds on her apron. "After you children see Colonel Travis, please go to the church. The Colonel has decided it will be the safest place for us to spend the night. Right now, I need to see if the other families are settled in." She brushed some loose hair away from her face and walked wearily away.

Once she was out of earshot, Bowie said, "Susannah's been the heart and soul of this old fort." Several men nodded at the comment.

The sight of a man walking across the courtyard interrupted the conversation. Hannah shook Nick's arm to get his attention. "He looks like the toy soldier I found in Mr. Barrington's trunk. Who is he?"

"He must be Colonel Travis," Nick replied.

"He's not in uniform," Jackie said.

"Look at the faces of the men," Nick said. "They know he's in charge."

Travis was wearing a heavy coat over a dark blue jacket, exactly like the toy soldier Hannah had found. A sword jingled at his side, and his eyes were bright with anticipation. He called out, "Men, gather around. There's something I need to say to all of you."

A hush came over the crowd as a group of men approached from all directions. At a motion from Bowie, several soldiers picked up his cot and carried him closer to Travis. Crockett and McGregor laid their instruments down and blended into the group.

Journey to the Alamo

Colonel Travis took a step forward. "I have gathered you all together tonight to remind you of why we are here." His voice carried to all parts of the Alamo. "There is a cry for freedom throughout this great land we call Texas. It can be heard from the Rio Grande River in the west to the piney woods out east, and we are the answer to that cry for freedom. We must remain true to our cause."

The courtyard was silent while Travis contemplated his next words. Hannah held her breath as she waited for him to continue.

"I also have unfavorable news to share with you. When Jim Bonham rode out from the gates of the Alamo on his way to Goliad, I had high hopes that Colonel Fannin and his four hundred men would join us in our efforts against the Mexican army. When Bonham returned, he informed me that Fannin and his men would not be coming to our aid."

Men's voices rumbled softly. "What happened?"

"Surely others will come."

Travis, aware of his soldiers' concerns, remained stoic. "It has been twelve days since this siege has begun, and I know the battle is almost upon us. I have great faith in all of you gathered here today. You are soldiers of exceptional courage. The time has come to test that courage."

Bowie coughed, and then motioned for Travis to go on.

"Men, I will never give up or surrender. And now you must decide your fate. Those of us remaining behind these walls will make our mark on the pages of history."

Colonel Travis drew his sword and walked proudly toward the last man. He put his sword to the ground. "I am drawing this line so you can make your choice." As he walked back, he dragged his sword, making a deep cut in the earth. "If you will stay and fight, step over this line. If not, may God be with you as you ride through the Mexican army to safety."

A murmur arose from the defenders. Crockett's voice rang out: "There's no decision to make, Colonel Travis. I'm for Texas!" He stepped across the line, and the others followed.

I'm for Texas, too, Hannah thought. She got to her feet and headed for the line in the sand.

Nick jumped up, grabbed her arm, and held her back. "He's not talking to you, Hannah. He's getting his soldiers ready to fight. It wouldn't be right for a seventh-grade girl to cross a line beside the Alamo defenders."

Hannah's gaze followed Travis. "His speech—it really touched me. Do you think people from our time realize what kind of leader he actually was?"

Nick pondered her question. "It's hard to say. People of the past can be forgotten."

"His words are almost like a gift," Hannah said as she sat down beside Jackie, "words that should be remembered."

Jackie patted Hannah's shoulder. "This might sound stupid, but I'm feeling very patriotic right now. If you had crossed that line, I would have been right behind you."

Hannah smiled at her best friend. No one would forget what had happened here tonight.

CHAPTER TWELVE

Colonel Bowie

Two men carried the cot holding Colonel Bowie toward a building next to the kitchen. As they passed by the campfire where Hannah, Nick, and Jackie were sitting, Bowie called out, "Hold on there, boys. Set me down for a spell. I promised Susannah I'd keep an eye on these young'uns."

Just then, Colonel Travis joined the group. "Jim, is there anything I can do for you? We need your strength when the Mexicans attack."

Instead of answering, Bowie coughed, trying to clear his throat. A noise rattled deep within his chest. "I won't allow this illness to hold me back. When the battle begins, I'll be ready. The freedom of Texas is there at our fingertips; I can almost touch it."

Another coughing spasm shook Bowie's body. Hannah rushed to his side and helped him sit up. She knew how it felt to be gasping for air. Bowie patted her hand and turned back to Travis. "Colonel, Susannah wants you to talk to these young'uns."

Travis's eyebrows drew together. "Crockett and I have maps to review, and there are dispatches to be sent. Send them to my office in an hour."

Bowie nodded. "All right boys, I'm ready to go inside. You three follow us." With a firm grip on the bed frame, the soldiers grunted as they hoisted Bowie up on his cot.

Hannah touched Jackie's arm. "Nick and I think Mr. Barrington's trunk is somewhere in the fort."

"Of course," Jackie said excitedly. "We open the trunk and poof, we're home."

Once they reached the room at the end of the building, Nick held the door open. The men entered first, set Bowie's cot down, and then left.

Hannah shivered in the drafty room. A wooden cross hung on the wall above Bowie. Looped over the cross was a white beaded rosary. A rickety table with paint peeling off in jagged strips stood next to the bed. On top of the table was an iron candleholder, branching out with five lit candles. Beside the candles were a pitcher of water and a dented tin cup. The trunk wasn't anywhere in sight.

Bowie tried clearing his throat. He leaned over the opposite side of the bed and coughed into a spittoon.

Hannah poured a cup of water and handed it to him. He took only a few sips and set the cup beside him. Nick pulled up two wooden stools for the girls, and he stood behind them.

Bowie studied Hannah's face. "My wife Ursula had your coloring and delicate features. She had those deep brown eyes, same as yours, same as our two boys." He paused to take in a couple of breaths. "Ursula's father was governor of Texas a few years back. He loved to entertain and have magnificent parties we call fandangos. Folks from all parts of Mexico would come and have a glorious time." Beads of sweat glistened across Bowie's forehead.

"Is Ursula here?" Hannah asked.

"Three years ago, my family came down with cholera." Bowie's voice wavered. "I lost them all—my wife, my boys, and her parents—all to that same appalling disease."

"That's so sad," Jackie whispered.

Bowie paused. "I miss them something fierce," he said, struggling to take in irregular breaths. "If Ursula and I had a daughter, Hannah, she would have looked a lot like you." Hannah wished she knew the right words to console him.

"Enough talk of my life," Bowie said. "Why don't you tell me about yourselves and how you ended up here? I don't recollect seeing any of you before."

Hannah glanced nervously at Nick. She had never been

good at lying, so she decided to change the subject. "Jackie and I have been friends for ages. We're in the same grade at school, Colonel Bowie."

Bowie pushed the blanket off his chest. "Who's your teacher? I know most folks around here."

Hannah felt herself panic. Another question she couldn't answer. Her mind was a jumble of information about the future.

"Ah . . ."

Nick nudged Hannah, signaling her to remain quiet. He said, "Colonel Bowie, I bet you were wild in your younger days."

Bowie chuckled. "My brother, Rezin, and I got in all kinds of mischief growing up along the Louisiana bayous. My poor mother had quite a time with us. We spent many long afternoons fishing instead of sitting in school." Bowie took another drink of water. "Rezin fashioned my famous knife. It's under the cot. See if you can reach it for me, Nick."

Nick bent down on his hands and knees to rummage around for the knife. "I can't see anything here," he said.

Hannah removed one of the candles from the holder and kneeled down on the floor beside Nick. Candlelight flickered, creating shadows that camouflaged everything beneath the bed. Arm outstretched, Nick swept carefully across the floor with an open palm. He continued until his fingers touched a leather sheath containing the knife. He grasped the weapon and brought it into view. Carefully, he pulled the knife out of its sheath, gawking at its sharp edge. It was over fifteen inches in length!

Bowie coughed again as his body shook. "You'd better give that to me, son." Nick placed the knife in one of Colonel Bowie's shaky hands.

"That's huge!" Jackie exclaimed.

Bowie said, "You have to realize where I was living at the time was an untamed area. And trouble had a way of finding me. This knife gave me an advantage. Today, every woodsman worth his salt carries one like this." Bowie cleared his throat. "I'm also known as a man tough enough to wrestle alligators!"

Jackie gripped the edge of her stool as she dragged it closer to Bowie. Her eyes widened. "Did they ever bite you?"

Bowie smiled as he set his knife down. "I only wrestled alligators over six feet in length. If they're any smaller, it wouldn't be a fair fight for the animal! Bring a candle over here, Hannah."

Hannah held the candle toward Colonel Bowie. He pushed up his sleeve. There on the outside of his forearm were numerous small scars in a curved line. Hannah, Nick, and Jackie were practically on top of the man as they admired the marks. "There is a story for every scar

I have, and there are many. Now, don't go feeling sorry for me. When the fight was over, I had a brand new pair of gator boots before the doctor had a chance to sew me up."

Hannah longed to hear more of Colonel Bowie's stories. She had forgotten all about the importance of going back to her own time. Refilling his cup, she asked, "Is there a doctor here?"

Bowie shifted on the cot. He trembled as a chill took hold of him. "Oh, he comes in from time to time. Not much can be done now except let this sickness run its course. Now, Hannah, tell me how you ended up here."

Hannah was trapped. What could she say?

Bowie focused on her until she squirmed under his gaze. "Are you keeping something from me?" Twisting around, he opened a drawer in the bedside table. He reached inside and withdrew a small carving knife and a portion of a branch. With a thoughtful look on his face, he started to whittle as flecks of wood fell aimlessly around him. "Let's have it."

Hannah turned to Jackie and then Nick. She stammered, "I—I can't lie to him. Let's tell him the truth. Maybe he can help us get home."

Jackie nodded in agreement, but Nick grimaced. "That's okay, Hannah," he said. "It was bound to come out." Nick looked anxiously at a silent Bowie. "This isn't our time. I mean, we're from the future. Hannah's school-teacher has a wooden trunk that's carved and painted with designs. When we opened it, we heard strange noises and smoke surrounded us."

Jackie added, "The next thing we knew, we were here."

"Now we don't know how to get home," Hannah said sadly.

Colonel Bowie stared at them in dismay for what seemed an eternity. The room was silent except for a wheezing sound Bowie made with each breath he took. Hannah knew their story didn't sound possible, and Bowie was definitely not pleased.

"I don't believe it," Bowie growled, "not one word. When you reach Colonel Travis's office, don't repeat that yarn you're spinning." He shouted out a command to someone outside the door. A soldier walked in and Bowie ordered, "Take them to Travis."

Hannah's head hung down in regret as they followed the soldier out of the room.

CHAPTER THIRTEEN

❦ ❦

Colonel Travis

The soldier led Hannah, Nick, and Jackie across the courtyard. Travis's office was centrally located along the west wall. A few campfires spread out though the grounds, burning for light and warmth. Some men gathered around the fires in two and threes while others slept at their posts. Hats and rifles jutted out as dark silhouettes along the walls. The Alamo had transformed into a place of unexpected peace.

Even though it was dark, Hannah could see a thatched roof over the building. The door was closed, and the soldier instructed them to wait outside until the colonel was ready. Muffled voices drifted through an open window.

When their escort left, they collapsed to the ground.

Nick and Jackie leaned their backs against the building. Hannah sat across from them, hugging her legs to her body. Her feet were hidden under her dress. She was confused over how to blend in when they were so obviously out of place. "We don't belong here, and now Colonel Bowie thinks we lied."

"It takes real courage to be honest with someone," Jackie said sympathetically. "These are honorable men. They expect the same of us. Colonel Bowie didn't know we did the honorable thing by telling the truth."

Nick patted the top of Jackie's head. "That was very deep thinking, Jackie. You do have something up there besides gossip and fluff. We just need to loosen it all up once in a while."

Jackie scowled at Nick, pushing his hand away. "I know absolutely everything about everybody at school. And it's all based on facts, not gossip."

Nick chuckled at Jackie's quick comeback. Hannah slid closer and stared at her brother. "You like teasing Jackie."

"She's so easy to rattle," Nick responded, suddenly serious.

Hannah moved even closer. "I wonder if . . ."

"Stop talking about me like I'm not here," Jackie insisted.

The voices on the other side of the door grew louder. Nick said, "Listen up. The Alamo falls on March 6th. We need to ask Travis today's date, and then figure out how to get home."

"The trunk could be in his office," Hannah suggested.

Jackie pulled Hannah to her feet. "If it's not, we'll have to search through every building. I've spent way too much quality time with your brother."

"You wish," Nick said.

Jackie scrunched up her face. "Eeewww."

The door opened. Crockett stepped out, followed by Travis. Hannah compared the two men. Both had long, bushy sideburns that would seem out of place in modern times. That was where the similarities ended. They were as different as two men could be. Travis, almost half the age of Crockett, was a serious and determined commander even without a military uniform.

On the other hand, Crockett seemed as casual as his buckskins. His slow, smooth manner of speaking and relaxed expression didn't give away any clues to what he was thinking.

"You have company, Colonel," Crockett drawled. "Be sure of this. My men are fired up and ready." With those last words, Crockett walked into the courtyard.

Another defender came out of the office. He was young, about the age of a college student. His black jacket fit loosely and was patched in several places. Under the jacket, he wore a striped vest and a white shirt. To complete his outfit, he sported a rumpled top hat resembling the one Abraham Lincoln wore.

Colonel Travis handed him a folded paper. "It's imperative this letter get through Mexican lines tonight."

The young man nodded. "You can count on me, Colonel," he said, sounding somewhat nervous.

"You're a good man, James Allen." Travis patted him on the shoulder.

Holding the letter firmly in his hand, James drew in a deep breath. "I'll return with help."

Moving toward the office window, Travis called out, "Joe, I have something important for you to do."

Joe appeared in the doorway and pulled his hat down on his head. "What you need, Mister Travis?"

"Saddle up the swiftest horse in the corral," Travis ordered, "and see to it that Allen gets off safely."

"Yes, sir," Joe said and headed into the courtyard.

Travis focused on James. "Keep a fast steady pace until you're outside of Béxar. Even then, keep your guard up. Don't take any unnecessary risks."

James slid the letter into a pocket. He buttoned up his jacket and walked briskly away. His expression showed no fear for the danger he was about to face, even though Hannah heard the uncertainty in his voice.

Colonel Travis turned to Nick. "I believe I'm ready for you children. Come into my office and tell me why Mrs. Dickinson is so concerned."

They followed Colonel Travis into a room that served as both office and personal quarters. He sat down behind a modest desk strewn with papers and military gear. On the right side, a spyglass stood on end, holding several maps in place. In the middle, an unfinished letter lay next to a bottle of black ink. A powder horn on the opposite side had a trail of gunpowder leaking from the tip. Slung over a chair in the corner were his heavy coat and hat. A military sword leaned against a wall in the corner next to a rifle and a shotgun. A narrow bed, similar to Bowie's, was against a wall, just a few steps from the desk. *No trunk in here,* Hannah thought.

They approached the desk and stood before Travis. The colonel took a sip from a tin cup. "Now, why are you here? I'm extremely busy, so let's get to the point." Colonel Travis didn't have time to be friendly like Bowie and Crockett. He was responsible for all the lives at the fort. Setting his cup down, he picked up a dark gray stone in one hand and a knife in the other. He spit on the stone and proceeded to rub the knife's blade against it in a circular motion, honing it to a razor-sharp edge. He worked the knife while waiting for a response.

Nick fidgeted with a loose button on his jacket. "We were separated from our parents when the Mexican troops marched into *san antonio de béxar*. Several families were coming here for safety, so we followed them. I have no idea where our parents are."

Hannah exhaled in relief. Nick handled lying better than she had, and Toribio's version of how they ended up here was the perfect solution.

Travis spoke up immediately. "It would be unwise to send you out with one of my soldiers in search of family members. There are far too many Mexican troops ready to prey upon any Texians, even young ones such as yourselves. That leaves us with only one alternative. You will report to the church and remain under the supervision of Mrs. Dickinson. Do you have any questions?"

"Just one," Jackie said, moving to the edge of the desk. She nervously traced a deep scratch in the wood with her fingernail. "I've misplaced my diary. I was wondering if you could tell me today's date. When I find my diary, I want to record it correctly."

Travis held up a thin black book. "I also have a journal. It's important to keep accurate records in the military. Today is the 5th of March." Setting the journal down, Travis got to his feet, grabbed his coat and hat, and started for the door.

Hannah shivered. She felt goose bumps rising up from the backs of her arms. March 6th was only a few short hours away. Would they find the trunk before the battle began?

Nick gripped Hannah's arm and pulled her out of the room. He muttered, "Let's go! We're running out of time."

Journey to the Alamo

CHAPTER FOURTEEN

The Ring

Hannah, Nick, and Jackie followed Colonel Travis to the church. Large statues of saints in flowing robes looked down with compassion from both sides of the doorway. Hannah stared at their faces. She felt as if they were judging her, deciding her fate. Feeling unbalanced, she took hold of Nick's arm to keep from stumbling over the uneven ground.

As they entered the building, Hannah tried to picture the Alamo she had seen during family trips to San Antonio, the Alamo of her time. It was hard to believe the church had survived, considering all the destruction around her now, in 1836. Most of the roof was missing. Broken pieces of limestone had been gathered and filled in with dirt to create a ramp leading upward. A dark sky blanketed the men at the top, giving them ghostly appearances. She could hear voices bantering back and forth as the men worked.

Travis trudged over the rubble and through a second doorway on the left side. This part of the church still had a ceiling. Once inside, Hannah admired a mosaic-styled border painted on the walls of the room. Regardless of everything she had seen, the building still held its mystical air. "The trunk has to be close by," Hannah murmured to Nick. "I can feel it."

Some family members of the defenders crowded the room. They were sitting on blankets in small groups about the floor. Lanterns and candles spread a pale glow over the faces of the women and children. The light accented their looks of desperation. Hannah wondered if her face was the same.

Jackie whispered to Hannah, "It's time for me to network. There has to be someone in this fort who has seen the trunk." Jackie walked to the center of the room and started talking to a woman, admiring her baby. At the same time, her eyes darted around as she examined every object.

Colonel Travis put a hand on Nick's shoulder, leading him and Hannah over to Susannah. "I am entrusting you with their care," Travis said.

"I'm happy to help out, Colonel," Susannah answered. A little girl, less than two years old, clung to her skirts. She playfully hid her face when Travis smiled at her.

"I see you, Angelina," Travis chuckled. He reached out and lifted her up. The child rubbed her eyes and yawned.

"She's always taken to you, Colonel," Susannah said.

Travis touched her blonde curls and tickled her neck. Angelina giggled. The colonel cradled her in his arms and laughed as the child reached up for his hat. "I wish I could spend time with my son, but holding this beautiful child close to my heart is the next best thing."

Nick and Hannah exchanged quick glances. They hadn't seen this side of Travis. He was a father, and he missed his son, a son he would never see again.

Travis asked, "Susannah, could you spare a thread from your sewing box? The color isn't of any great importance." Susannah nodded and hurried off on her errand.

Travis turned to Nick and Hannah. "This babe in my arms is the reason we are fighting for the freedom of Texas. Our children will have a better life because of the sacrifices we have to make."

"How old is your boy?" Hannah asked.

Travis smiled at her. "Charlie, he's almost seven. He's staying with friends of mine."

Susannah returned with a long dark string. Travis gave Angelina one more look and handed her back to Susannah. The woman's expression touched Hannah. Susannah's eyes were moist, but she held her chin high, refusing to let her emotions show.

Travis remained steadfast. He slid a gold ring off his

finger. It had a black cat's-eye stone set on the front. After guiding the string through the ring, he tied the ends together in a knot, creating a necklace. "I would like to give this ring to your daughter in remembrance of me and all the brave Alamo defenders. She's part of us all now, and this ring will symbolize our fight for freedom."

He slipped the necklace over Angelina's head. The weight of the ring caused it to fall and rest gently on her chest. Angelina clasped the heavy ring in her hand and cooed.

Susannah's eyes glistened. "Thank you, Colonel Travis. As soon as Angelina is old enough to understand, I'll tell her about all of you."

Travis touched the brim of his hat. "I must get back to work. There are a few unfinished letters on my desk. You're a brave woman, Susannah."

Hannah felt a lump in her throat. *He's saying good-bye. He knows what's about to happen.*

As Travis walked away, Mrs. Dickinson turned her attention to Hannah and Nick. "Find a spot and settle down for the night. I'll get some blankets for you."

Hannah and Nick decided on a corner away from the other families and sat on the floor. While leading a small boy by his hand, Jackie dragged a colorful quilt over and dropped it beside them. The boy's eyes were wide as he stared from Nick to Hannah.

"He's so cute," Hannah whispered, touching his dark curly hair. "How old are you?"

The small boy proudly lifted up his arm. He held out three fingers.

Jackie knelt down on the quilt. "His name is Francisco."

Nick smirked. "Time to give the kid back, Jackie. He's not a souvenir."

"I wanted to, but Mrs. Esparza asked me to keep an eye on him for a few minutes," Jackie hissed. "By the way, the trunk isn't here."

"What now?" Hannah sighed.

"Hey Franky, how's it going, dude?" Nick laughed.

Francisco walked over to Nick and stared at him. The little boy reached into his pocket. When he took out his hand, he held it toward Nick in a clenched fist.

"What's that?" Nick asked.

Francisco slowly opened his fist. There was something silver in his palm. Nick took a dime-sized coin from Francisco's hand. "The words aren't in English, and the year is 1794. That's old." Nick flipped the coin up in the air, caught it, and handed it back to Francisco.

"Again," Francisco demanded, as he offered the coin to Nick.

Nick flipped the coin into the air, higher this time. Francisco's eyes followed the spinning coin, and he clapped when Nick caught it. "Again," Francisco said eagerly.

Nick shook his head and muttered, "That's it for babysitting. I'm out of here. I'll check through the barracks for the trunk. As soon as I find it, I'll be back."

"But—" Hannah interrupted.

Nick scrambled to his feet. "We have to find the trunk. I'll blend in with the guys, Hannah. You won't in that dress."

"Nooo!" Francisco stamped his foot when he realized Nick was leaving.

"Here, Hannah." Nick tossed the coin to his sister. "You entertain him."

As Nick walked through the doorway, a boy entered. He was a few years younger than Nick, and he resembled Francisco. The boy's pants were short for his height. There was a light line several inches above the bottom edge of his pants, marking the original hem. The cuffs on his sleeves didn't reach his wrists. He approached the girls. "Why is Francisco here?"

"Mrs. Esparza asked me to watch him while she took food to her husband," Jackie explained. "Who are you?"

"I'm Enrique, his brother." Francisco ran to Enrique and began to run around him.

"Is your father a defender?" Hannah asked.

Enrique nodded, struggling to hold Francisco still.

"His name is Gregorio. He is helping Jim Bonham with a cannon that's up there." He nodded toward the ceiling. "I want to fight next to my father, but he says I am too young."

"So your whole family's here," Hannah said. "That's kind of scary."

"It was a hard decision for my father to make." Enrique sat down and forced Francisco to stay in his lap. "My uncle is in the Mexican army. He predicted that everyone behind these walls will be killed. My uncle begged my mother to stay with him, but my mother refused to leave my father's side."

"Your mom is fearless," Hannah admired.

Jackie's mouth dropped open as she leaned forward. "Your father and his brother are on opposite sides. That means they have to fight each other!"

Francisco squirmed until Enrique released him. The young boy ran to Jackie and planted himself in her lap. "Agh, he's heavier than he looks," Jackie winced.

"My father is a very religious man," Enrique said. "He prayed for guidance. At first, he used to argue with my uncle about Mexico returning to the 1824 Constitution. He says things about Santa Anna and how he took away some of our rights. I think he no longer wants *tejas* to be a part of Mexico, but it is hard for him knowing my uncle is on the other side of those walls."

"Enrique," Hannah said, "since I've been here, I've

heard the words *Texian* and *tejano.* They kind of sound the same."

Enrique explained, "I am proud to be a *tejano.* That means I live in *Tejas,* which is a part of Mexico. Sometimes new settlers call themselves Texians. Those two words mean the same thing. Colonel Travis calls himself a Texian."

By this time, Susannah Dickinson was coming in their direction carrying more blankets. She set them on the floor next to Hannah. "These should help keep out the cold. Enrique, your father has asked for you."

Enrique quickly rose to his feet and smiled at Hannah and Jackie. "*Vamonos,* Francisco." He gripped Francisco's hand tightly.

"Wait," Hannah said. She handed the coin to Enrique. "This belongs to Francisco. I'm not sure how much it's worth."

Enrique took the coin and looked at it. "It's a half *real.* My uncle gave it to him for luck. Francisco is favored by my uncle since they share the same name."

Francisco waved to the girls as he followed Enrique out the door.

Susannah kneeled down beside Hannah. "Where's Nick?"

"Uh . . . he went outside," Hannah said.

Susannah took Hannah's hands and held them in hers. "You need to prepare yourself."

"What do you mean?" Hannah asked.

"Unless reinforcements arrive soon, the Mexican soldiers will scale those walls. Your brother might be considered an Alamo defender. Make sure he stays in here with the families. It could save his life."

"Could?" Jackie squeaked.

"We live in hard times," Susannah said as she got up to leave.

CHAPTER FIFTEEN

No Long Good-byes

"What could have happened to Nick?" Hannah asked nervously.

"Don't worry," Jackie said. "He's been gone so long, he probably found the trunk . . . or maybe not."

Nick quickly came through the door, followed by a man with a sour expression. The man leaned against the doorway and watched Nick walk away from him. "Now you stay in here, boy," the man ordered. "Don't let me catch you outside again." The man turned and left the room.

"Whatever," Nick muttered. He sat down beside Hannah and exhaled loudly.

"What happened?" Hannah asked.

Nick scowled. "That guy caught me going through the

barracks. He yelled at me like a little kid, told me I was getting in the way, told me, 'It's past your bedtime, sonny.'"

Jackie giggled. "You are kind of young to be a defender."

"Go ahead and laugh, Jackie. We'll see how funny it is when you face those Mexican soldiers tomorrow. I've been through every building here. And guess what? There's no trunk." Nick stood up and started to drag away a blanket.

"Wait," Hannah said. "I have to tell you what Susannah said."

"I don't want to hear it, Hannah." Nick moved to a dark corner. He tossed the blanket over his shoulders and stretched out on the floor, his back to Hannah.

Hannah curled up in her blanket, watching her brother doze for what seemed like hours. Jackie slept soundly to the side of her. Hannah tried to close her eyes, but they wouldn't stay shut.

A hand touched her shoulder, gently shaking her. *"¡Levántate! ¡Levántate!"* Enrique insisted.

Hannah turned over. "Huh?"

"Wake up! *Señor* Bowie has asked for the three of you to come to his room, *pronto*! He has something *muy importante* to tell you."

Hannah crawled over to Nick with Enrique right behind her. Her brother could sleep through just about anything. "Nick," Hannah yawned, shaking his arm.

"You have to wake up. Colonel Bowie wants to see us."

Nick rubbed his eyes groggily. "What time is it?"

"It's very early," Enrique responded. "You need to hurry. *Señor* Bowie is demanding to see you right now!"

Nick sat up, moving his blanket aside. "What does he want?"

Hannah rubbed the side of Jackie's head, waking her. "Oh no, we're still here?" Jackie moaned. "I thought I had a really, really bad dream."

"We need to go to Colonel Bowie's room," Hannah whispered. "Try to be as quiet as you can."

Only their own soft footsteps could be heard as they hurried out of the church into the darkness. Enrique warned them not to wake his mother. She would never allow them to leave the safety of the church.

There was a chill in the air, and clouds drifted across the sky, covering the moon. An uneasy stillness filled the courtyard. The cannon and musket fire had ceased hours ago. Most of the Alamo defenders rested quietly at their stations, waiting for whatever was to befall them.

Hannah glanced at the spot where Travis had stood, inspiring his men. She would have crossed that line with the soldiers if Nick hadn't held her back. Maybe this was what Mr. Barrington wanted all along. History had come alive for Hannah, and her view of the past would never be the same.

Journey to the Alamo

"Come on." Jackie tugged on Hannah's arm, pulling Hannah in the direction of Bowie's room. A light drizzling rain fell upon her face, bringing her thoughts back to the present. If Nick was correct, this would be the day of the Battle of the Alamo. How could the three of them stand against the entire Mexican army and survive? They had to find the trunk and find it fast.

After they passed by the kitchen, they hurried into Colonel Bowie's room. Bowie spoke anxiously to Enrique, "*Gracias, amigo,* for bringing them so quickly. Now, Enrique, tell them exactly what you told me."

"*Sí,* there is an unusual trunk stored in the room with the gunpowder. It is painted with many colors. I saw it when I was there with my father."

Hannah's heart stopped. That had to be Mr. Barrington's trunk!

Bowie said, "Now don't take offense, Enrique, but I need to talk to these young'uns alone. There's a private matter we need to discuss."

Enrique nodded respectfully. "I should take water to my father. *Señor* Bowie, do you know why it is so quiet?"

Bowie's face showed his concern. "It's eerie, son. I don't like it one bit, not one bit."

After Enrique left, Nick and Jackie stepped closer, and Hannah sat on a stool. Colonel Bowie took Hannah's hand in his and looked at her. He paused before he spoke, taking short irregular breaths between coughs. His eyes were bright with fever. "I still can't get over how you remind me of those who are lost to me," he confessed sadly. "It's those soulful brown eyes."

Hannah shivered. Now every time she looked at herself in the mirror, she would think of what Colonel Bowie had said. Never again would she see her eyes as plain, flat brown.

Bowie reached into a pocket on his shirt. He pulled out something small enough to fit in the palm of his hand. "Hannah, I'm sorry if I upset you earlier. Life can sometimes take unexpected turns." He opened his hand and showed her a finely carved cross, similar to the one hanging over his bed. There was a slight hole in the top with a white satin ribbon threaded through it. "I want to give you something to remember me by." He knotted the ends before placing the ribbon over her head.

Hannah grasped the cross in her hand. "Thank you. I'll never forget you." Her eyes felt moist as she gazed at the dying man.

A lone tear found its way down her cheek. Bowie reached up to brush it away. He spoke tenderly, "No time for tears, Hannah. Be brave for me."

Bowie turned to Nick and said, "I've been contemplating that unbelievable story you told me. Maybe it was the fever, but I started thinking that you just might be telling the truth. Then Enrique mentioned seeing a trunk. Well, if you are from the future, I have a few questions needing answers, tonight."

Nick, Hannah, and Jackie exchanged nervous glances and nodded in agreement.

Bowie shifted, trying to get comfortable. "You don't have to tell me what's about to take place. It's obvious. I need to know what our last stand will mean to the future of Texas. Are these brave men about to die for a reason, or will we be forgotten?"

Nick took a step closer to the cot. "The battle goes down in history, Colonel Bowie. You're in all the Texas history books, along with Crockett, Travis, Seguín, Bonham, and the others."

Bowie sighed as Nick continued. "A few weeks from now, Fannin and his men will be slaughtered at Goliad, but Sam Houston eventually leads the Texians to victory against Santa Anna during the Battle of San Jacinto. When it's over, Texas will be a free nation. Houston becomes the first President of Texas."

"Good ole Sam," Bowie mumbled with a faraway look in his eyes. "He'll make one hell of a president."

"The Alamo is eventually made into a shrine. People from all over the world will come to see it," Nick said. "In front of the Alamo is a huge stone monument in memory of the heroes who died there. Your names are engraved on it."

"You'll always be remembered," Hannah added.

For the first time, Colonel Bowie appeared completely relaxed. "Then we won't die in vain. We will make a difference in Texas!" He smiled at them while he squeezed Hannah's hand.

"One last question, and don't be afraid to answer it," Bowie added. "Do I die like a hero, or from this confounded sickness? There's no reason to hold back now."

Jackie jumped right in, her face animated. "When I was in fourth grade, I did a report on you, which, by the way, I received an A for. In one of my library books, I saw an illustration of you during the battle that I will never forget as long as I live. You were in bed because of your sickness, of course. When the Mexican soldiers entered your room, you were ready for them. That dangerous knife was in one hand and a pistol in the other."

Colonel Bowie smiled and coughed at the same time. Once he caught his breath he said, "I wouldn't have it any other way. Dawn will be here soon, so it's time to finish our affairs," he said firmly. "I have a bad feeling in my gut that our time is short. I don't want you three in here when the Mexicans breach the walls."

Nick asked, "Where's the gunpowder stored?"

"It's right there in the church on the northwest side. Good luck getting home."

"Can we get you anything?" Jackie asked as she straightened out his blankets on the bed.

Bowie shook his head. "No long good-byes. We all have our destinies to fulfill, and I have accepted mine. Nick, I expect you to take care of these two young ladies. It's your duty to keep them safe at all costs. The Mexican soldiers are seasoned fighters. Do you understand?"

Nick nodded. For the first time in his life, Nicholas Taylor was speechless. Both Hannah and Jackie had heart-broken expressions. They would surely miss their new friend, and they couldn't do anything to stop the battle that was about to begin.

Before leaving, Hannah and Jackie propped Bowie up on several pillows until he was in a sitting position. Nick handed him a knife and two pistols. Then he set plenty of ammunition on the bed within the man's reach. Hannah touched Bowie's arm as a last farewell. No more words were spoken. Jim Bowie's time on this earth was coming to an end. They slowly left the room, afraid to look back; Hannah held the wooden cross firmly in her hand.

CHAPTER SIXTEEN

⚞⚟

The Battle

As Hannah, Nick, and Jackie reached the door, musket fire crackled and popped like a thousand firecrackers. A soldier shouted, "Man your posts and prepare for battle!"

Troubled about leaving the safety of the building, they paused outside as Jackie closed the door. Hannah remembered what Susannah had said—the Mexican soldiers would see Nick as the enemy.

A bloodcurdling scream cut through the air. Jackie jumped back against the building. She held up her watch and pressed a button to illuminate the face. "It's barely 5 A.M.! How can they see what they're shooting at?"

"We have to be brave like Colonel Bowie told us," Hannah advised confidently. "And we're wasting time. We need to find the trunk and get home!"

Jackie and Nick looked at Hannah. She was different. Only days ago, Hannah had been reluctant to start school. Now she had the courage to step out onto the battleground, not knowing what she would face.

"This place has changed you for the better, Hannah," Nick said. The siblings exchanged a quick smile as they entered the courtyard.

Hannah clutched Nick's sleeve and led him away from the building. He shook his arm loose. "Let go. I'm not a little kid crossing the street."

"But we need to hurry," Hannah urged.

Cries of "Viva Santa Anna" floated over the walls. Shouts from all directions bombarded their ears as soldiers raced through the fort. High up on the walls, the defenders fought frantically for their lives. Terrifying screams came from *soldados* trying to scale the walls as the Texians shot them down, one at a time. The acrid smell of gunpowder filled their lungs, causing Hannah to cough.

Hannah, Nick, and Jackie stood in awe at the horrendous scene. One defender rushed at them. It was Galba. He had an expression on his face that showed his itch for adventure had been replaced by fear and uncertainty. He shouted, "Hide yourselves! The Mexicans are upon us!" Too stunned to speak, they watched as Galba bolted back across the grounds. Hannah stared at Nick and froze.

"Come on, Hannah!" Nick shouted. He grabbed her

arm and pulled her along. Nick kept both girls moving toward the church as they dodged the defenders racing through the courtyard.

By the light of soaring rockets, Hannah caught sight of a familiar hat on the north wall. Colonel Travis stood beside a cannon, calling out orders to the men around him. Suddenly his voice stopped, and he plummeted to the ground. "He's been shot!" Hannah gasped in horror.

Crisp bugle calls reminded them that they were almost out of time. They ran at full speed through the smoky air. Hannah noticed David Crocket at the palisade wall, right where he said he'd be. David hollered, "We have 'em in our sights, boys! Stay the course!"

A cannon blast rocked the earth. Sparks from the artillery weapons streaked through the blackened sky. "Hurry!" Hannah screamed as they approached the double doors of the church.

One defender stood in the entryway. He seized Hannah and Jackie by their arms and forced them into the room with the families. Nick was right behind his sister. "Stay in here!" the man growled as he rushed off.

The room was filled with terrified people. Women huddled with their children in close family circles. A baby cried, frightened by the noise. Susannah came forward, carrying Angelina. "Praise be, you're safe. Enrique told me you were with Colonel Bowie."

Nick put his arm around Hannah. "My sister's not feeling well." He tapped Hannah's shoulder, and she began coughing.

"The smoke is bothering her," Jackie said. "Maybe it would be easier for her to breathe over there." She pointed toward a darkened corner of the room.

Susannah patted Angelina's back. "The three of you need to remain inside. Before long, I may need your help with the wounded." Nick and Jackie nodded while Hannah coughed one last time.

Shifting Angelina to one side, Susannah reached into her apron pocket. She removed three stubby candles and handed them to Hannah before she moved toward the doorway.

There was a small table up against the wall with a single burning lantern. Hannah lifted the glass dome, and Jackie lit the candles. Nick took one candle and located the Esparza family. He wanted to ask Enrique about the trunk.

Hannah and Jackie hurried to the corner of the room. There was very little light given off by the candles they carried. Hannah noticed a gap in the wall, exposing an opening that led into another room. "This wasn't here before," she said. It looked like the stones had shaken loose from the vibrations of cannon blasts, creating a jagged doorway. Holding their candles in front of them, Hannah and Jackie hunched over and peered inside.

Hannah felt a hand on her shoulder and tensed up. It was only Nick. "Enrique says the trunk is in there," he said. Nick knocked away a few more stones and gave both girls an encouraging push into the next room.

"Hey, watch it," Jackie grumbled, stumbling through the opening. She aimed her candle at Nick and shook it as he eased himself through the hole. "You're not the boss, you know."

"Be careful with the candle," Nick warned. "There's enough gunpowder in here to blow us all up. There'll be pieces of us scattered all the way back to Austin."

Jackie frowned as she quickly turned her candle to an upright position. "You think you're *so* smart, don't you?"

"That's a no-brainer," Nick teased.

Hannah quickly gripped the back of Nick's jacket. "Come on! Let's find the trunk."

"Yeah, whatever. Split up," Nick said, "and watch out for spiders, Jackie."

"Aahh!" Jackie exhaled.

Setting off in different directions, they each began a desperate search for their way back to the future. Every wooden surface had to be inspected for carved and painted designs.

Hannah followed a path until she was completely surrounded by boxes piled up so high, she could no longer see Nick or Jackie. Glancing down, she noticed a child's toy.

Someone must have misplaced this, she thought. It was a doll with blond ringlets and a soft body. Hannah straightened out its dress and thought of Angelina as she touched the ceramic face.

BANG! BANG! The gunfire was getting closer. It sounded like hail pelting the church walls.

"Help!" Jackie cried. Hannah retraced her steps until she found her friend.

Nick raced from the opposite side of the room. "What happened?"

Jackie was noticeably upset and trembling. "It was awful. It's so dark, I didn't even see them." Hannah put an arm around Jackie as they sat down on a box.

Nick grumbled, "Get to the point, Jackie!"

Hannah gave her brother a threatening glare. "Don't be rude. She's upset." She turned to Jackie. "Tell me what happened," Hannah coaxed.

Shivering, Jackie took a deep breath. "These—these nasty mice scurried over my feet. I think I stepped in a nest of them. It was *so* creepy!"

Disgusted, Nick stared directly into Jackie's eyes. "It's not like they have fangs, Jackie. Get over it!"

Hannah handed Jackie her candle and headed straight at her brother. "That's enough," she snapped. She grasped the doll tightly, threatening to swat Nick with it.

With a smirk, Nick snatched the doll away and tossed it

The Battle   119

to the floor. It landed with a thump next to Jackie's feet. "Mom's not here to save you this time," Nick sneered. "What's your next move?"

Hannah bent down to pick up the doll. "This is probably Angelina's." As she turned, she noticed the box Jackie sat on wasn't shaped like the others. She quickly ran her hand along the side, brushing off dust and dirt from its surface. What she uncovered was ancient, and had carved and painted designs. "Jackie, you're sitting on Mr. Barrington's trunk!"

"What?" Nick exploded. He crouched down to take a closer look. "And you didn't see this?"

Jackie stammered, "I—I hadn't noticed." She stood up and held the two candles in front of her to get a better look. "It's the trunk, all right."

"Those are real guns out there with real musket balls slamming into the building, Jackie," Nick growled.

"Duh, like I don't know that," Jackie replied.

Hannah forced her way between Nick and Jackie, putting an end to the argument. She tried to lift the latch on the trunk, but it wouldn't open. There was a lock on it! "That wasn't there before!" Hannah gasped. She jiggled the lock, but it wouldn't give way.

Nick reached over and tugged at the lock. "We need some sort of tool to break it. Our lives might depend on it."

Jackie called out nervously, "Attention all mice, clear the area!"

BOOM! The roar of a cannon jolted them into action.

Nick went one way and the girls another. Hannah and Jackie bent down on their hands and knees and felt around in the partial darkness. They passed several wooden crates and turned left. "There's something behind this keg," Jackie said. "I have it!"

Getting to their feet, the girls hurried back to the trunk. A shiny hatchet glimmered in Jackie's hand.

Nick grinned at Jackie and nodded. "Not bad for a mouse magnet!" Jackie handed him the hatchet like a peace offering.

It took Nick only two hard blows to break the lock. A cheer bubbled up from both girls. Nick snapped up the latch, and Hannah opened the lid. A soft shimmering sound of vibrating cymbals could be heard. With a sigh of relief, they all peered inside. Disappointment covered their faces. The trunk was empty!

﹄﹃

CHAPTER SEVENTEEN

The Forgotten Clue

Hannah clutched the cross around her neck. The sound of cymbals had stopped. "There's nothing inside the trunk, and we're still here!" she cried.

BOOM! The cannon on the roof fired. The walls shook with such force that a powdery coat of dust floated down on the frantic trio below. Outside, heavy gunfire continued while the battle raged on with a life of its own. They could hear muffled shouts from the defenders through the thick walls of the church.

Jackie paced frantically across the floor, deep in concentration. Her long skirt swished with every step she took. She mumbled each fact over and over that had led to their appearance at the Alamo.

Hannah walked to the opening in the wall and checked on the families in the next room. Fearful children were huddled around their mothers. Susannah tried to comfort her daughter. A pink-faced Angelina cried softly on her shoulder. Hannah knew it wouldn't be long before Mexican soldiers stepped through the front door of the church. When that happened, none of them would be safe.

Jackie took Hannah's arm and rushed back to the trunk. "There must be something we overlooked," she muttered. She kneeled down to inspect the inside. Reaching in, she ran her hand along the shadowy bottom. Hannah lowered a candle close to the trunk, and Nick joined Jackie in the search. The cannon on the roof blasted away, causing plaster to rain down from the ceiling.

Jackie brushed off powder from her face. "I think I found something." She took out a piece of paper and unfolded it. It was torn; a portion of the top part was missing. The edges were wrinkled and brown. "It's hard to understand this old-fashioned handwriting with all those curlicues. This seems to be a list of supplies: six maps, one spyglass, one buckskin jacket, one powder horn, four journals, twelve miniature soldiers . . ."

Nick interrupted Jackie before she could finish. "That's what should have been in the trunk! Look at the name on the bottom. It says 'D. Barrington.' Finish the letter, Jackie."

It was too late. The thud of heavy footsteps pounded outside, followed by shouting voices in the church. A musket fired in the room where the families were hiding. Someone screamed.

"I think people are dying out there!" Hannah exclaimed. "What do we do now?"

"Blow out your candles!" Nick yelled.

All three crouched beside the trunk in total darkness. Hannah could hear a whirling, clicking sound nearby. "What's that?" she whispered in a shaky voice.

"It's only the wheels on the Corvette from the cereal box," Nick whispered back. He was quiet for a moment.

"Huh?"

"What now?" Jackie hissed.

"I found something, but it's too dark to see it," Nick said. "Wait a minute. The only things I might have put in my pocket were the car and the . . ."

Hannah eagerly finished his sentence, "The figure of the Alamo! Remember when we were in Mr. Barrington's room? You put it in your pocket right after you . . . Open the doors so we can go home!"

Angry soldiers yelled in Spanish at the people in the next room. "Hurry, Nick!" Hannah begged.

"Got it!" he exclaimed.

The familiar and welcome sounds of soft shimmering cymbals began. The smell of smoke came from the trunk.

Hannah stood up. She took hold of Nick's and Jackie's hands. They formed a small circle so no one would be left behind.

Sounds of stones breaking off and falling to the floor came from the corner of the room. Hannah looked back through the haze at a glowing light growing larger. A Mexican *soldado* held a lantern before him as he crawled through the hole in the wall. Hannah could see blood splattered over his uniform. She screamed as a second *soldado* hustled around his comrade. He held his musket high, the bayonet aimed toward them. The soldier's expression was fierce and terrifying. He moved forward, locking his eyes with Nick's.

"No!" Hannah cried. Using all her strength, she grabbed Nick's arm and pulled him away from the soldier.

The noise from the trunk grew deafening, and suddenly everything turned black.

CHAPTER EIGHTEEN

⇥⇤

What Really Happened?

Hannah heard voices and felt a hand massaging her shoulder. She opened her eyes and saw Nick by her side. "We're alive?" she asked groggily.

Nick grinned. Hannah looked around at the familiar classroom until she saw Jackie was safe as well.

The school nurse, Mrs. Santos, and Mr. Barrington approached her. Mrs. Santos kneeled beside Hannah, felt her head, and applied an icepack. "You have quite a bump back here. Do you feel dizzy?"

"A little," Hannah mumbled.

"Can you stand with our help?" Mrs. Santos asked.

Hannah agreed as the nurse and Mr. Barrington eased her up. She was surprised to see a broken limb from the fallen tree had shattered the window. It reached so far inside the room that it partially covered the teacher's desk. Shards of glass were scattered across the windowsill where toy soldiers had once stood at attention.

"We had quite a storm this afternoon," Mr. Barrington commented. "I'm relieved you're not severely injured. It certainly made a mess of my desk." He pulled over a chair so Hannah could sit down.

The nurse took out a stethoscope and listened to Hannah's heart and lungs. "Your breathing is normal. You must have been knocked out by the falling branch."

Hannah looked at the clock on the wall. It was 4:30. School had only been out an hour. That was impossible! What was happening?

The nurse interrupted her thoughts. "I called your mom. She should be here any minute." Mrs. Santos walked to the window, observing the damage caused by the storm.

Mr. Barrington sat next to Hannah. "Are you positive you're all right?"

Hannah adjusted the icepack. "I'm a little mixed up. That Mexican soldier was right there. The cannon fired so loud, it hurt my head. How did you ever survive, Mr. Barrington?"

Mr. Barrington looked puzzled. "There aren't any soldiers at school. Perhaps the storm sounded like a cannon. You were here working on research, remember?"

Hannah's heart raced. "You played the fiddle while we danced by the campfire. We became part of history, just like you wanted. And you were there at the Alamo with us, as David Crockett. Only you pretended not to know me."

Mr. Barrington smiled. "It sounds like you'll write an imaginative research paper, exactly what I wanted. It must have been an exciting dream, but that's all it was. You're confusing what you read with what really happened."

Mr. Barrington rose from his chair. "Keep an eye on her," he said, patting Nick on the back.

Nick nodded. "No problem, Mr. Barrington."

Jackie took Mr. Barrington's place next to Hannah as Nick paced around the classroom. She whispered, "Our teacher is so weird. Are you really all right?"

Hannah nodded. "I'm fine. Am I the only person here who remembers our trip back in time to the Alamo? Have I gone completely crazy?"

Jackie and Nick glanced at each other, but remained silent. Before Hannah could ask another question, her mother hurried into the room.

"Are you hurt, honey?" Mrs. Taylor called out, rushing to Hannah's side.

"I'm fine, Mom," Hannah said. She was starting to feel embarrassed by all the attention.

Nick walked up behind Hannah. "And Nick, it's nice of you to be here for your sister," Mrs. Taylor added.

Nick shrugged.

"Hi, Mrs. Taylor," Jackie said.

Mrs. Taylor smiled at Jackie. Then she lifted up the ice pack and gently felt her daughter's head. "What a bump!"

"Let's just go home," Hannah replied sullenly.

As they walked through the school, Mrs. Taylor chatted away like a mother hen. Hannah was afraid to ask any more questions. Nick and Jackie hadn't said one word about the experience they shared. Was Mr. Barrington right? Could a sharp blow from a broken branch put all those wild ideas in her head? But she remembered everything so vividly. She tasted the steaming hot stew with Crockett, she witnessed Travis draw the line in the sand, she felt Bowie hold her hand, and she heard cannon fire, not just the roar of thunder. It was all so real!

When they reached the school's parking lot, Jackie's mother was just driving up. Jackie said, "Bye Hannah, talk to you tomorrow." She gave Hannah and Nick one last worried look before opening the car door.

The Taylors climbed into their Suburban and headed for home. Nick kept avoiding Hannah's questioning glances. She waited for him to say something, but he only turned his head away and stared out the window. Hannah could hear a clickety-click as Nick spun the wheels on his Crispy Car.

Later at home, after Mrs. Taylor fussed over Hannah

and tucked her in bed, Nick appeared in her doorway. "Come in," Hannah said. "I need to talk to you."

"Mom ordered me to leave you alone," Nick said as he crossed the darkened room and sat on the bed next to Hannah. "You have a big lump on your head. I guess that means I'm supposed to be nice to you." He picked up an overstuffed teddy bear from the floor and tossed it to her.

"What happened? Did we really travel back in time?"

Nick reached over, gently grasping a white ribbon from around Hannah's neck. He gave it a slight tug, and out came a wooden cross from underneath her shirt.

Tears welled up in Hannah's eyes as she remembered Colonel Bowie placing it around her neck. She ran a finger along the length of the cross. "This is the proof! We were there at the Battle of the Alamo!"

Nick flashed one of his famous smiles. "It was some journey."

"Why didn't you say anything? You should be bragging to the world about our adventure."

Nick grabbed the bottom of his T-shirt and lifted it up from one side. He turned around so Hannah could see a thin red gash about three inches long beneath his left shoulder blade. A narrow scab had formed over the wound. "I almost got shish kebabbed, Hannah. When the Mexican soldiers ran toward us, I wasn't so sure I'd make it. The last thing I felt was the razor-sharp tip of a bayonet in my back. If we'd been there any longer . . ."

"Wow, that was close," Hannah said in awe. The corners of her mouth turned up a tiny bit. "It would've been lonely here without you."

"Lonely, baloney," Nick sputtered. "And don't think I've forgotten about our deal. You owe me your allowance for opening that trunk."

"Half," Hannah corrected.

"Nicholas!" Mrs. Taylor shouted from the hallway. "I told you to leave Hannah alone so she can rest!"

Nick straightened out his shirt. "One more minute!" He rolled his eyes and said, "She kind of reminds me of Toribio. 'Nick, do this,' and 'Nick, do that.'"

Hannah giggled, thinking about Toribio's heels clicking across the floor.

Nick reclined on his side and used the teddy bear for a pillow. "On top of Mr. Barrington's desk, hidden under all those branches, was an old fiddle with a bow. A red fox tail was tied to one end of the bow just like David Crockett's. I'd like to hear your teacher explain that one away."

Hannah's eyes opened wide. "There wasn't any fiddle or bow in the trunk when we went through it."

Hannah and Nick smiled at each other. They both knew exactly what that meant. "Tomorrow, Mr. Barrington and I need to have a little talk!" Hannah said.

"Count me in, Hannah Banana," Nick added. "Who knows what else we might find in his trunk?"

SPANISH TO ENGLISH TRANSLATION

(First time a word appears)

꒦꒷

CHAPTER 7

Dios mío: my God

está bien: very well

entiendes: do you understand

las cebollas: the onions

mija (mi hija): my daughter

mijitas: my daughters

mijo (mi hijo): my son

norte americanos: North Americans

señor: mister

señora: Mrs.

señoritas: young ladies

sí: yes

solamente niñas: only children (girls)

Chapter 8

coahila y tejas: Coahila and Texas
de nada: you're welcome
gracias: thank you
soldados: soldiers

Chapter 9

tejano: Texan

Chapter 14

real: Spanish coin
tejas: Texas
vamonos: let's get going

Chapter 15

gracias amigo: thank you friend
levántate: get up
muy importante: very important
pronto: quickly

Spanish to English Translation

ACKNOWLEDGMENTS

⊰⊱

Writing this book has been an extraordinary journey. My love of Texas history combined with the support of good friends has enabled me to see this journey through to the end.

Special thanks go out to Judith Keeling and Dr. Jan Seale. Judith, my editor at Texas Tech University Press, gave me the advice and encouragement necessary for a first-time author. Jan shared her talent for writing, helping me see the world through Hannah's eyes.

Many thanks to the historians who offered their expertise during this project: Dr. Richard Bruce Winders, Curator of the Alamo; and Dr. Alwyn Barr, Texas Tech University.

Thanks to the patient readers who were willing to page through my early stages of this story: Dora Elizondo Guerra,

Daughters of the Republic of Texas Library, Retired; Tony Cuate; Marcy Saenz; Christina Garza; and Ray Gardner; as well as later readers.

I appreciate all the help I received from Martha Utterback, Daughters of the Republic of Texas Library; and Katherine Dennis and the staff at Texas Tech University Press.

One final thank you goes out to all the students at Canterbury Elementary School. Let history become your adventure!

Acknowledgments